E-mail from: Mitch [illegible]
Turning Point, Texas [illegible]
To: Dan Egan, fire chief, Courage Bay, California

Sky's gray, rain's starting to come down and the main roads are jammed with traffic. Hurricane Damon is on its way to Texas.

Haven't got much time, Dan, but I wanted to let you know your crew arrived safely—the least I can do after you sent me four of your best to help out. One day I hope to return the favor—but what would California's finest emergency team need from a small-town fire chief?

I picked up the four this morning at Corpus Christi airport and they've jumped right in to help. We're hoping we just have to deal with a flood of evacuees, but having a doctor, nurse, paramedic and EMT handpicked by you sure makes me feel better.

I've already sent out the paramedic with my daughter to see to a woman in labor. Nate Kellison looks as if he could handle just about anything. Jolene figured she could go on her own, but no father would let his pregnant daughter set off in this storm alone—even such a determined and capable girl as my Jolene.

Gotta run, Dan. The wind's really picking up now. I'll keep in touch unless the power's off. Don't worry about us down here. You know we Texans are tough. Just say a prayer Hurricane Damon realizes that and heads back out to sea.

About the Author

CODE RED

JULIE MILLER

attributes her passion for writing romance to all
those fairy tales she read growing up, and shyness.
Encouragement from her family to write down those
feelings she couldn't express became a love for the
written word. She gets continued support from her
fellow members of the Prairieland Romance Writers,
where she serves as the resident "grammar goddess."
This award-winning author and teacher has published
several paranormal romances in addition to her
beloved romantic suspense. Inspired by the likes
of Agatha Christie and Encyclopedia Brown, Julie
believes that the only thing better than a good
mystery is a good romance. Born and raised in
Missouri, she now lives in Nebraska with her
husband, son and smiling guard dog, Maxie.

CODE **RED**

JULIE
MILLER

RIDING THE
STORM

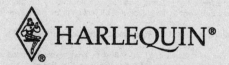
HARLEQUIN®

TORONTO • NEW YORK • LONDON
AMSTERDAM • PARIS • SYDNEY • HAMBURG
STOCKHOLM • ATHENS • TOKYO • MILAN • MADRID
PRAGUE • WARSAW • BUDAPEST • AUCKLAND

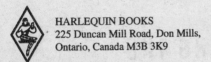

HARLEQUIN BOOKS
225 Duncan Mill Road, Don Mills,
Ontario, Canada M3B 3K9

ISBN 0-373-61296-6

RIDING THE STORM

Copyright © 2004 by Harlequin Books S.A.

Julie Miller is acknowledged as the author of this work

www.eHarlequin.com

Printed in U.S.A.

Dear Reader,

I grew up in the heart of America's Tornado Alley, so when Harlequin asked me to write a story set in the midst of a hurricane, I almost panicked. I mean, when was the last time a hurricane hit the flat plains of Nebraska?

When I put out a help message on the loops, I received several responses from friends and fellow writers. One grew up on the Texas Gulf Coast, another survived Hurricane Andrew, and yet another talked about East Coast hurricanes. The coolest part was that every person I contacted was willing to share personal stories—funny, graphic, inspiring and practical.

By the time I'd completed my research, I felt I could give my story an authentic tone. I had the facts about heavy rains and scary winds and spooky calms. But I could also imbue my characters with realistic reactions and emotions. I could *feel* that hurricane coming to life.

So as you read *Riding the Storm,* keep in mind all the real-life stories and adventures that went into creating the characters and the disaster they must survive. A few of you might even see something familiar.

Stay warm and dry—and enjoy!

Julie Miller
www.juliemiller.org

PROLOGUE

"KELLISON. YOU AWAKE?"

Paramedic Nate Kellison scrubbed the sleep from his eyes and blinked at the clock on the bedside table into focus: 10:00 a.m.

"Yeah?" he snapped into the phone.

It was an amazingly civil response, considering he'd just gotten home late from a thirty-six hour sleepless shift with the Courage Bay, California, Fire Department an hour ago. A shift where he'd worked several car wrecks and a house fire. A shift where he'd helped save a handful of lives—people whose names and faces blurred in his sleepy memory except for one little girl. Her features had been serene and unblemished, even as he'd unbuckled her dead body from the car seat and tried to resuscitate her. That tiny face was etched as clearly as a photograph in his mind, and Nate knew it would stay there forever.

"Dan Egan here."

Nate sat up, springing to attention. Troubling thoughts were instantly pushed aside as he answered the call to action as surely as he did every time the alarm sounded. "Chief. What's up?"

"I know you had a rough shift and should be asleep." Chief Egan's gruff concern put Nate on alert.

Caution dampened the adrenaline sparking through each nerve ending. Surely his boss hadn't wakened him to offer condolences or counseling. The department had a counselor on hand for that kind of stuff. And Nate had his family to turn to if the emotional baggage got too heavy to deal with.

Or rather, he used to have a family to turn to.

Grandpa Nate had been gone for years now. And his older brother and sister, Kell and Jackie, had moved on to families of their own. Nate glanced around the small bunkhouse turned studio-style apartment. Hell. This wasn't even a home for him anymore. It was just a place to sleep between his shifts with the fire department and work on the ranch.

"I'm okay, Chief." Nate scratched at the dark, stubbly growth of beard on his jaw, and tried not to feel anything as he asked the next question. "You're not calling to tell me the mother in that crash didn't make it through the night, are you?"

"No. She's still in stable condition at the hospital. They've located the father and he's with her right now. Last I heard, the chaplain's there, too." Last he heard. Nate almost smiled at that one. Dan Egan had probably just gotten off the phone with the hospital. The man was nothing if not thorough.

"So why'd you call me in the middle of my beauty sleep?"

The chief laughed. But when he spoke, his words were deadly serious. "I just got a call from an old buddy of mine in my hometown of Turning Point, Texas." Nate knew the chief was a transplanted Texan. "We used to work together at the fire department there. He was a mentor of mine—about five years older than me. He taught me the ropes about fighting fires and public safety. His name's Mitch Kannon."

"Sounds like a good man."

"The best."

Sensing the urgency in Dan's voice, Nate flipped back the sheet and swung his legs over the side of the bed. The shiny scars from reconstructive knee surgery after he'd shattered his right leg eight years ago gleamed against his tanned skin. "So what does Mitch Kannon want from us?"

He could imagine Chief Egan's grin. "You're reading my mind, Kellison."

"That's why they pay me the big bucks."

"Your best talent is your reliability. I know I can count on you, no matter what situation I throw you into. And I've got a doozy for you this time."

Nate was wide awake now. "So what do you want to throw me into?"

"Mitch has a hurricane headed his way. He's looking for medically-trained volunteers and supplies to man an emergency station for Corpus Christi residents being evacuated to Turning Point."

Nate remembered seeing reports on the national news of the tropical storm forming out in the Atlantic and picking up strength as it headed into the warmer waters of the Gulf of Mexico. "Hurricane Damon, right? Don't they have disaster procedures in place?"

"They do. But Mitch is in a tight spot. The town's only doctor had a heart attack a couple of weeks ago and is recuperating at a hospital up in Houston. He had one licensed EMT, but she just got married and moved to

North Dakota to be with her husband. All he has is a group of volunteers—some with basic medical and emergency training, some not. He's got plenty of stubborn Texas horse sense, but even that won't get him too far on his own."

"He doesn't have anyone he can call for backup?"

"He called me."

That said a lot about the strength of Dan's friendship with Mitch Kannon. As a result, Nate extended a degree of respect and loyalty to this man in Texas he'd never met.

Nate didn't even have to be asked. He rose to his feet.

"When do you need me?"

CHAPTER ONE

A LONG, LOW SCREEN of pearl-gray clouds clung to the horizon over the Gulf of Mexico in the distance, refusing to surrender to the sunrise. Mist drizzled in the air, hanging like a translucent shroud and muffling the world outside.

Nate absently massaged the dull ache in his right knee and took note of his surroundings. Despite the jostling and jarring of the Chevy Suburban he rode in, the morning seemed unnaturally still. Way too still for his peace of mind.

The chatter from the five souls inside the official white vehicle provided the only signs of life in the middle of this vast stretch of flat scrub land. Where were the birds, winging to the sky, searching for the proverbial worm? Where were the tiny rodents, scurrying from cover to cover as the snakes and other nocturnal predators turned in for the day?

Wise enough to protect her own, Mother Nature wasn't waking up this morning. She knew something Nate could only sense.

Turning Point, Texas, was a disaster waiting to happen.

Apparently, Nate, who'd taken the red-eye flight from California to Corpus Christi with the other three volunteers, wasn't the only one to think so.

"All hell's gonna break loose." Turning Point's Fire Chief, Mitch Kannon, a friendly, authoritative man, reminded Nate a lot of his own boss. Though Mitch had a bit of gray peppering what was left of his short brown hair, both he and Dan easily carried the weight of responsibility on broad, sturdy shoulders.

Mitch glanced across the Chevy's cab and shook his head like a weary father trying to make sense of a recalcitrant child. He looked into the rearview mirror to include the three women who'd volunteered for this mission along with Nate. "I've been watching Hurricane Damon on the radar for a week now. Having Corpus Christi send their evacuees down to us is a mistake in so many ways—the scenario reads like a comic strip."

Clearly, Mitch wasn't amused. He had driven to Corpus Christi to pick up the California team and had been dismayed at the caravan of cars already heading south to Turning Point. As they left the main highway now, he turned his steely blue gaze back to the road that would eventually take them into town. "What am I going to do with a thousand extra people in my town?" he complained.

Nate braced his hand against the dashboard and watched the flat plains, just forty miles inland from the Texas Gulf Coast, zip past. Though the terrain was more brown than green, and trees stood at a premium in the sandy soil, he recognized good ranch land. Not unlike the quarter-horse ranch in Southern California where he'd grown up. Where he'd buried his parents before he was old enough to remember them. Where Grandpa Nate had raised him, and left a little bit of his wise old soul inside him. Where he and his older brother and sister, Kell and Jackie, had formed a bond that had seen them through hell and back.

Where he no longer had a home.

Nate shut down that disturbing train of thought and shifted in his seat, trying to alleviate the stiffness in his knee. The old injury had been acting up more than usual the past couple of days—probably due to fatigue. He felt uncharacteristically restless. But not about the job at hand. Never about the job. He'd always been able to shut off his emotions when it came to the business of saving lives. "You don't have the facilities to handle that many evacuees?" he asked.

"I don't have the facilities, the supplies or the manpower to handle Damon and whatever he decides to throw at us." Mitch rubbed at his receding hairline. "Turning Point is a small, rural town. Times like this, it doesn't seem as if it's changed all that much from when the pioneers first settled here in the 1880s. Right about now I'd happily exchange our *quaint and historical getaway* reputation for a fully-staffed, state-of-the-art hospital and a couple of interstate highways to get people in or out of here as fast as we need to."

"Well, we can't build a new highway for you overnight." Nate shrugged, trying to ease the older man's concern. "But we'll do whatever we can to help."

"I appreciate it." Mitch slowed the Suburban as he neared an intersection. "I wasn't sure Dan could deliver when I called and asked for help. But he promised he was sending his best."

The look Mitch slid Nate indicated he'd be holding them to that promise.

"Yes, sir."

Mitch stopped at the intersection to let three cars pass. Though a skyline of low rise buildings indicated the town was in view several miles to the east, the older man gripped the wheel in both hands and stared down the road to the west. Nate turned his head to see what had captured his attention. But the black asphalt ribbon, long and empty, faded into the mist.

Nate glanced back, noting the lines of strain bracketing Mitch's mouth. "Is there a problem?"

"No." Mitch expelled a long, shaky breath, then turned and headed east. "My daughter lives out that way. On the Double J Ranch. Hopefully she's got enough sense to stay home today." Hopefully? Mitch didn't sound convinced that *sense* and *daughter* belonged in the same paragraph. "I'll call her from the station house. Make sure they're okay."

They. Son-in-law? Grandchildren?

Before Nate could ask another question, Mitch turned on the Suburban's siren and lights. Resolutely burying any hint of concern about his daughter and her family, Mitch sped around the three cars and headed into town.

Always the careful observer, Nate shoved his blue fire department ball cap back on his head and peeked inside each vehicle as they drove past. Fleeing the oncoming storm, the cars were loaded down with suitcases, pet carriers, boxes, clothes, food—and a baby strapped into a car seat. Thank God the infant carrier was facing the proper direction in the back seat.

Nate took a deep, silent breath to ease the tightness that clenched his stomach. He couldn't afford to go there right now. Forcing himself to stay in the moment, he studied the evacuees inside the cars. They wore every expression from dazed to determined to downright scared.

He'd never witnessed a hurricane before, but in his career he'd dealt with fires, earthquakes, mudslides, and way too many traffic accidents. He recognized the faces of trauma. These people had been uprooted from their homes, chased out by forces beyond their control.

Nate knew the feeling.

He reached into his pocket and rubbed the plain gold wedding band he'd inherited from his grandfather. Carrying the gift for all these years hadn't exactly been a lucky charm for him, but it was a link to the past. A link to family ties that were changing faster than he could adapt.

With Kell and his wife Melody living on the ranch in California, there was no longer a need for Nate to hold down the fort while his brother worked odd hours as a mounted police officer. And after a disastrous first marriage, ending in her husband's suicide, his sister had finally found a good, solid man to love in Casey Guthrie. Jackie no longer needed Nate's shoulder to cry on. She had a husband to listen to her troubles now.

Hell. There were no more troubles. Not for Kell, not for Jackie. After their grandfather's death, Kell had been the father figure. Jackie had looked after their home. As the youngest sibling, Nate had wound up being the listener—a sounding board for his brother and sister. But the role that had defined him for so many years had eroded beneath his feet.

He'd have to deal with his own troubles now.

Almost like an empty-nester, Nate felt alone for the first time in his life. All the personal relationships he'd knowingly or subconsciously put on hold in order to be there for his family and friends had passed him by. It was time for him to move on—like the evacuees seeking a haven in Turning Point from the approaching storm.

But like that fictitious man without a country, Nate felt adrift at sea. His future seemed uncertain, and except for his work as a paramedic, he'd yet to find anything to spark his passion or earn his loyalty enough to convince him to make a change.

Nate plucked at the collar of his dark blue uniform shirt and settled his cap down over his short, dark hair. He turned his focus back to the older man beside him. Enough self-analysis. His personal life might be in a state of flux right now, but his work had always been there for him. And right now, his work was here in Texas. As self-appointed leader of this band of volunteers, it was his responsibility to have all the facts in place so their team could make the most efficient use of the supplies they'd brought, and utilize their skills and talents where needed most.

"It was my understanding that the hurricane's due to make landfall sixty miles northeast of here." Nate didn't have to be psychic to sense the older man's tension. "But you sound as if you're expecting casualties."

"I'm expecting anything and everything," Mitch said. "You should, too. My old bones are sending me a different message than the weather service." *Old* was a figurative term, Nate decided. Mitch Kannon couldn't be a day over fifty. And though he was apparently well-fed, the stocky fire chief was in good shape. "Mark my word. That storm's gonna turn."

"You think the hurricane will hit farther south, closer to us?" came an energized voice from the back seat.

"Will we be able to see it this far away from the coast?" Dana Ivie, a firefighter and EMT who worked at the Courage Bay station with Nate, was known for her enthusiastic approach to her work. "I've never seen a hurricane before. Except on TV. Now I wish I'd brought my camera."

Nate couldn't hide his indulgent smile. He and Dana had shared more than one middle-of-the-night chat over a cup of coffee at the station house, relishing the excitement and bemoaning the hazards and heartbreaks of their chosen career. "You've never seen an avalanche or tornado before, either," he teased. "Maybe you'd like to take the scenic route on the way back home."

Dana laughed. "Very funny, Kellison. I'm trying to have a positive attitude here. I'm looking at this thing as an adventure, not a tragedy waiting to happen."

"I hope you're right." Mitch didn't sound convinced. He killed the siren and stopped at what appeared to be one of the town's few traffic lights, then turned right past a sprawling brick building easily identifiable as a school. They slowed as they passed the football field and headed toward a residential area. "We plan to put up as many evacuees as we can here at the high school. If that doesn't hold them all, then we'll have to ask people to open up their homes. My brother-in-law, Hank, owns the hardware store downtown. He's donated all the cots, sleeping bags, lanterns and water jugs he has on hand. Beyond that, the townsfolk have pitched in blankets and pillows and food. We kept some at the firehouse, but like I said, we're nowhere close to being able to provide for a big influx of evacuees."

"Sounds like you have a real sense of community here in Turning Point."

Nate cocked his head to make eye contact with the brunette seated behind him. Cheryl Tierney, a trauma nurse from Courage Bay Hospital's E.R., was as detail-oriented as Dana was impulsive.

"But if your evacuees are scattered all over town, we won't have a reliable way to track them," Cheryl pointed out in her ever-practical tone. "And since we're not familiar with the area, we could be delayed trying to answer individual calls. Wouldn't it make more sense for us to set up at the school instead of in town?"

Mitch shook his head. "I've scheduled a briefing for you down at the firehouse at 8:00 a.m. I'd like to ask you and Dr. Sherwood to set up a triage center at the station." Amy Sherwood was the fourth volunteer from Courage Bay. "That'll free up Kellison and Ms. Ivie to handle the more routine calls. I'll give you a tour of our facilities, such as they are, and a map of the county. Right now, all our emergency calls come through the station, so we'll use that as our command post. As we get the weather updates, we'll have a better idea of what we're facing and whether or not we need to move to an alternate site."

"Will we be meeting your staff then?" Cheryl asked.

Mitch huffed a sound that wasn't quite a laugh. "My *staff* consists of a dozen or so volunteer firefighters who are scattered around the county right now, shoring up their own homes and making sure their families are safe. We'll see who shows up for the briefing."

Volunteers. Who might or might not show up for duty assignments. Who might or might not be properly trained for the potential range of emergencies brought on by a hurricane.

Reassuring? Hardly. Nate stared out the window to hide his scowl. No wonder Mitch had had to call Chief Egan for backup. This had to be the craziest, most haphazard, seat-of-the-pants rescue operation Nate had ever been a part of.

Dr. Amy Sherwood, a first-year E.R. resident at Courage Bay Hospital, raised her voice to be heard from the third seat. "Chief Kannon, perhaps you could tell us a little more about what to expect, weatherwise, with a hurricane."

"I will if you call me Mitch." He paused to turn on the wipers, clearing the condensing moisture from the windshield. "Damon is classified as a category four hurricane. If he hits Corpus Christi and the northern Gulf Shore like he's supposed to, we'll miss the brunt of the one hundred thirty to hundred fifty mile-per-hour winds."

"Whoa!" Dana's expletive said it all. "Maybe I don't want to see a hurricane, after all."

Mitch answered with a told-you-so shrug. "Generally August gets pretty hot and sticky around here. But if you noticed the chill in the air, that's the barometric pressure dropping ahead of the storm."

That explained the ache in Nate's knee.

"Joy and rapture," Dana groaned.

Amy knew what had triggered the sarcastic remark. "Ah, yes. The barometric pressure drops and pregnant women near their term go into labor. Remember the storm that hit Courage Bay a couple months back? We delivered three babies in the E.R. that night."

Nate remembered it well. He'd brought in one of the mothers who'd gone into premature labor. Mitch's white-knuckled grip on the steering wheel warned Nate that their temporary boss didn't find Amy's story amusing.

"I hope to hell you're wrong about that," the fire chief muttered.

Mitch turned onto a wide road aptly named Main Street. Though it was nearly deserted at this hour of the morning, the number of businesses—in brand-new buildings as well as remodeled historic structures from the early 1900s—indicated this was the town's commercial hub. A few of the storefront windows had been boarded up, but more had been left uncovered in defiance of the hurricane.

Or, in spite of Mitch's gloomy prediction, in the belief that Damon would stay true to his predicted course and blow past this sleepy little town.

They passed a tiny, stone-walled library and redbrick post office. Then Mitch pointed to a two-story, white-washed building with a Closed sign hanging in the window. "That's our clinic. Generally, our maternity cases go into Alice or Kingsville. Or, if there are complications, we fly them up to Corpus Christi. But I don't have an ambulance or driver to spare to take anyone anywhere right now. And nobody's flying north. Nobody's flying anywhere once the heavy rains hit. So no babies, got it?"

"We'll tell the mothers to cross their legs until the storm blows over, okay?" Even Mitch smiled at Dana's ludicrous suggestion.

As they stopped at a crossroads near the center of town, Nate turned the conversation back to practical in-

formation about the hurricane. He was feeling more responsible by the minute for his team's response. "When
you say heavy rains, how much are we talking about?"

The light turned green and Mitch drove on toward the
half brick, half vinyl-sided building with lettering that
read Turning Point Fire Department. "Six to ten inches,
on average, from the outer bands or leading edge of the
storm. Sometimes thunderstorms or even tornadoes spin
off inland along the storm's track as well."

Mitch pulled into the parking lot in front of the building. He pointed out the garage doors marking the three
bays where Turning Point's emergency vehicles were
stored. "We've got one ambulance and two engines, all
fully-equipped. But most of our volunteers use their
own vehicles when responding to a call. I'll make sure
you're partnered up with someone who knows the area.
Or I'll let you use the Suburban and give you directions
if it's here in town."

Parking by the front door, Mitch killed the engine.
The first ominous drop of water plopped onto the windshield with a portentous splash. All five of them stared
at the tiny puddle for an endless moment.

The storm was on its way.

Nate wondered if he should trust the dull throb in his
rebuilt leg the way Mitch seemed to trust his instincts.
If that was the case, he had a feeling this was going to
be one very long, very wet day.

The second raindrop hit. Then the third. Soon there
were too many to count. Like an alarm bell, the sudden
change in weather spurred the five travelers into action.

Nate adjusted the bill of his cap low on his forehead
and opened the door. The cleansing scent of ozone filled

his nostrils as he inhaled a deep, recharging breath and mentally prepared himself for the *anything and everything* Mitch had warned them about.

He circled to the back of the Suburban and met Mitch, who'd opened the doors to start unloading supplies. A splash of rain hit the bill of Nate's cap and dampened his cheek. The light shower seemed deceptively gentle. "Looks like things are pretty dry around here. I imagine a heavy rain could lead to some flooding?"

Mitch nodded, balancing three crates against his stocky chest. "The Agua Dulce River flows south of town, straight into the Gulf, so we might get some backflow from the storm surge. Plus, we've got a web of lakes, creek beds and man-made irrigation ditches crisscrossing the farmland and ranches west of here. I'm expecting a few road washouts, especially in the countryside."

"Is there high ground we should direct people to?"

"These are the flat, Texas coastal plains. High ground around here is the back of a horse or a rooftop."

Nate was beginning to understand Mitch's skepticism about Corpus Christi sending its evacuees to Turning Point. He grabbed three more crates and followed the chief inside, past the front office and dispatch room. Things weren't improving. Both rooms stood dark and empty. Where was Mitch's crew? This had to be the craziest disaster preparedness setup he'd ever seen.

Mitch flipped on a light switch as they entered a large room, which appeared to be a general meeting area. Cabinets, shelves and a small kitchenette lined one wall, and tables and chairs were scattered about the room. Following Mitch's direction, Nate set the crates down on one of the countertops and followed the chief back outside, passing Dana, Cheryl and Amy in the hall along the way. Each carried equipment and supplies.

"I can read the doubt in your eyes." Mitch might be a blustery worrywart, but Nate had already realized he possessed a lot more depth than his good-ol' boy facade let on. "You're thinking we're some backwash little town with more heart than common sense."

"I didn't say—"

"I'll have you know we've got an ample supply of both."

Mitch shoved a couple of paramedic kits into Nate's hands. "We aren't as slick an operation as Dan runs back in California. We don't have the resources or the personnel that you're used to. And, yeah, I'm worried. This is my town and these are my people who are at risk."

He picked up the last kit himself and closed the vehicle doors. When Mitch stopped to look him in the eye, Nate realized the barrel-chested man stood as tall as his own six feet. "But make no mistake. We're tough here in Turning Point. Resourceful. My staff might not have your formal training or wear a uniform or keep a regular schedule. But when the chips are down, you can rely on 'em."

The pride and certainty in Mitch's tone and posture brooked no argument. Whatever doubts this man had about the storm—about the next several hours of this dull, drizzly day—he had none regarding the people of his community.

Nate wasn't sure if the chief's remarks had been a dressing-down or a pep talk, but he got the idea.

Maybe he should have a little faith, too.

"All right." He nodded his head in lieu of a salute. "I promise I'll keep an open mind about the way you run things here in Texas."

"Just do your job, Kellison." Mitch's gruff expression eased into a grin as he headed for the station door. "Just do your job."

"Not a problem."

The splash of tires over wet pavement ended the discussion. Nate turned at the sound of two quick honks of a horn and saw a dark green, extended cab pickup truck zip into the parking lot. The driver of the pickup spun into a space opposite Mitch's Suburban and jolted to a stop.

Nate admired the brawny truck while bemoaning the merciless treatment of its shocks. "Looks like your first volunteer."

"Oh, no." Mitch didn't sound nearly as relieved as a man in dire need of help should be when the cavalry started to arrive. "No, no. Not today, baby."

Baby?

Mitch shoved the paramedic kit into Nate's already full arms and hurried over to the truck, where a sunny-haired woman in a pair of baggy overalls and scuffed-up Lacer boots climbed out. Instead of politely excusing himself and joining the rest of his team inside, Nate stayed on the front sidewalk and adjusted his load, half-hidden by the translucent mist as he watched the scene unfold.

He was scoping out the volunteers he'd be working with, he rationalized. Staying close to offer Mitch whatever backup he might need, since this woman's arrival had obviously upset him. Nate narrowed his gaze to take note of every detail that weather and distance allowed him to assess.

The woman wore her butterscotch cream hair pulled back in a straight, practical ponytail. The long strands hung past the collar of her man-size, bright green polo shirt. She might be a tad on the skinny side, though her bulky clothes and above-average height could be playing tricks on his perception. She had a definite spring to her step.

And quite possibly the bluest eyes he'd ever seen.

As she circled to the rear of the truck to greet Mitch, her face came into sharper focus. Nate's fine-tuned senses responded with something more than curiosity. Her eyes were as cool and blue as a pristine mountain lake. She was pretty enough, he supposed, in an unadorned, girl-next-door kind of way. But those eyes made her unforgettable.

How could her arrival be a bad thing?

"Hey, Dad." She braced one hand on Mitch's shoulder and rose up on tiptoe to exchange a kiss. So this was the daughter from the Double J Ranch that Mitch had been worried about.

"Honey, we talked about this." Mitch made a move to hug her or halt her, but she'd already stridden beyond his reach en route to the passenger-side door.

"I know. But I also know how short-staffed you are right now."

"I recruited help."

"Right. The California contingency. Sun-babes and surfer dudes."

Surfer dudes? Nate frowned. Was that a joke or an insult? He hadn't been on a surfboard since he'd blown out his knee, and phrases like *totally rad* and *gnarly* had never been part of his vocabulary.

"You know Dan would only send his best."

Her ponytail bounced as she nodded. "I know Uncle Dan's dependable, but you yourself said we were going to be shorthanded. So I'm here to volunteer for whatever job you need. Oh, and I passed Micky Flynn and Doyle Brown on the way in. They should be here soon."

"I'm glad some of my firefighters are finally showing up, but—"

"Here. Do you mind?" She leaned in and pulled out a large flat box from the passenger seat. Once she handed the package off to her father, she propped her hands against her hips, rolled her shoulders back and stretched, tipping her face to the rain and breathing deeply, as if she found the cool drops a soothing comfort. "Mmm. I love this moisture. My garden's going to love it, too. Everything's so dry."

"Now, honey, you know damn well that…"

The rest of Mitch's warning got lost in the pounding alarm stopping up Nate's ears. Her arched posture had pulled her loose clothes taut.

She was pregnant. Maybe four or five months' worth, judging by the subtle yet distinctive swell of her belly. Mitch was going to be a grandpa. No wonder he wanted her to stay home.

The blue-eyed angel with the nonstop mouth was pregnant.

The attraction humming through Nate's body braked into regretful silence. He didn't need to be lusting after somebody else's woman.

Wait a minute. *She was pregnant?*

A familiar sense of urgency buzzed his senses back on full alert.

She was Mitch's idea of a volunteer?

Every doubt that had been temporarily laid to rest resurfaced.

No wonder he'd called Dan Egan for help.

"I figured Aunt Jean's Café wouldn't be open this morning." Mitch's daughter pulled a second box from the truck, then closed the door with a subtle wiggle of her hip. She was smiling. Beaming like a ray of sunshine, despite the rain, the clouds and her father's scowl.

"So I got up early and baked some cinnamon rolls for the briefing this morning. If I know you, you didn't eat any breakfast." She winked. Nate zeroed in on the movement, fascinated by her animated expression and the spell she seemed to be casting over her father. "And I know you. C'mon. Let's eat one while they're still warm. I made them without nuts the way you like them. I'll brew some fresh coffee to go with them, too."

She hiked the box higher in her arms and marched across the parking lot, heading straight toward Nate and the front door. Mitch's big shoulders expanded with a sigh before he fell into step behind her.

"Promise me, all you'll do is make coffee and then go home?" Mitch asked.

But Nate had a feeling the concession had fallen on deaf ears. Mitch's daughter glanced up at the sky, arcing the slender column of her throat. "Maybe I'd better get the urn out and fill it up. I imagine we'll have people in and out all day who'll be looking for something to warm them up if this rain hangs on."

Nate barely got the door open for her before she

came charging through. She tipped her chin and gave
him a smile, which, even at a fraction of the wattage
she'd shown Mitch, was still dazzling. "Thanks. I'm Jolene Kannon-Angel. You must be the California boy
Dad told me about last night."

California boy? Surfer dude? "Nate Kellison."

He was too stunned by her exuberance, which somehow managed to intrigue yet condescend at the same
time, to do more than utter his name.

She didn't give him time to say "pleased to meet
you," set her straight on the whole California miscon-
ception, or tell her how good those rolls smelled. She
breezed on by, leaving a waft of cinnamon and a void
of energy in her wake.

Mitch paused in the open doorway beside Nate, staring after her retreating backside with openmouthed exasperation. "That's my daughter," he announced
unnecessarily. "She didn't stay home." He turned to
Nate. "I didn't really think she would. But I hoped. She
does have some medical training. She's been a volunteer firefighter for eight years now—since she was
twenty. She's as passionate about her hometown as I am.
She's good with people."

The credentials petered out as Jolene disappeared into
the main room. They could hear a chorus of cheerful greet-
ings as she introduced herself to Dana, Cheryl and Amy.

"She's pregnant." Nate stated the obvious. "Her
volunteerism is commendable, but she doesn't need to
be here."

Mitch nodded. "Yep."

"Isn't her husband worried about her being on the
road by herself?"

"She hasn't got one." That bit of news finally seemed to shake Mitch free from the lingering effects of Hurricane Jolene. "She's been a widow four months now."

A knot of compassion twisted itself in Nate's gut. He knew more than he wanted to about losing someone he loved. "I'm sorry to hear that."

"It's probably a good part of why she worries about me so much. She lost her mother years ago. And now Joaquin." Mitch led the way down the hall. "Probably why I can't say no to her, either. I don't want her to lose anything else. I don't want her to hurt anymore."

Nate supposed he could understand a father wanting to protect his daughter. Still… "You might not be doing her any favor by letting her work today. Does she have a friend's house where she can stay to ride out the storm?"

"You don't know my daughter." Mitch muttered a frustrated curse that was more of a growl than an actual word. "I'm beginning to think you four might be the only thing standing between us and…oh hell, I'm not even going to say it."

He didn't have to.

No doctor. No EMT. Not enough supplies. No volunteers except for one pregnant, widowed woman with more energy than sense.

And one powerful, unpredictable storm that could turn a routine evacuation into disaster.

CHAPTER TWO

JOLENE SAT AT THE DESK in the dispatcher's office, licking the sticky sweetness of her second cinnamon roll from her fingers and drinking her carton of milk.

She'd dashed in to answer the phone twenty minutes ago and wound up with a full-time job. Ruth, their regular dispatcher, hadn't made it in yet, so Jolene had redirected the inquiry about Hurricane Damon's projected path to the weather bureau. Then she stayed put to field three more phone calls from volunteers reporting in with their ETA's, and one from a Corpus Christi resident asking for directions to the high school evac site.

Answering phones rated at about a negative two on the excitement scale—she'd much rather be doing than sitting. But as she'd told her father, she was here to do whatever needed to be done. The people of Turning Point were her family as much as Mitch was.

Needing to fill the temporary lull, she swiveled the chair around to watch the gathering meeting through the glass window that separated the dispatch office from the station's commons area. A handful of locals had arrived for the briefing and had quickly dug into rolls and coffee, greeting their out-of-state guests.

The town's resident hot-shot pilot and fellow volunteer firefighter, Micky Flynn, had swaggered in a few minutes ago and was already trying to make time with the three female medical personnel from California. Jolene was slowly revising her opinion of the sun-in-the-fun crowd she'd expected her Dutch uncle, Dan Egan, to send from the Golden State. Cheryl, Amy and Dana were definitely babes, she supposed. Each woman was pretty in her own way. But they seemed friendly and competent and unafraid of hard work.

The man who'd flown in with them, Nate Kellison, was definitely more standoffish. Taking a swallow of milk, she searched the perimeter of the commons area. As she peered over the rim of the carton, she spotted him on the far side of the room, discussing something with short and squatty Doyle Brown.

Or rather, Doyle was talking and Kellison was nodding his head.

He didn't have a handsome face—the nose was a little too crooked, the jaw a little too square—but it was undeniably compelling.

A smile would help ease the tension bracketing his mouth. But she got the feeling Nate Kellison didn't smile much. Not recently, at any rate. A sprinkling of lines beside his eyes indicated smiles and laughter had once come easily to him. But there was something almost Atlas-like in the gravity surrounding him. For a man who couldn't be more than thirty, he seemed to carry a heavy weight of responsibility on his shoulders.

"What's your secret, Kellison?" she mused out loud.

He'd taken off his ball cap, giving her a better view of his ultrashort crop of coffee-dark hair and a chance to gauge the color of those unsmiling eyes. They were a dark, golden-brown, reminiscent of the fine sippin' whiskey her father liked to drink from time to time.

Those brown eyes blinked. When they opened again, they were focused on her. Dead on. Staring with an almost psychic intensity that said he'd known she'd been watching him. Startled at being caught, Jolene swallowed an entire mouthful of milk, forcing the liquid down her throat in one gulp.

There was something coiled and canny and downright unsettling in those whiskey-colored eyes.

But she couldn't look away.

Why was California Boy staring at her?

Jolene defiantly tipped her chin and held his gaze, ignoring the inexplicable clutch of nervous energy tightening her chest. She knew she didn't turn the heads of too many men—they were more likely to call her to set them up with a friend or bemoan their woman troubles than to ask her out herself. And she was okay with that. She had plenty of friends of both sexes to fill up her time. She had other people to give her heart to—her father, her baby, her hometown. They would always need her.

Joaquin had needed her. In some ways, he was the only man who ever had. And even with his big, generous heart, her husband had never given her more than his trademark bear hug or a platonic kiss.

Of course, he'd been so sick.

They hadn't even made their baby in the traditional way.

Automatically Jolene slid her hand down to cup the gentle swell of her belly, protecting that most precious part of her from any hurts the world tried to throw at them. Kellison's brown gaze dropped to follow the movement of her hand. Jolene flattened her spine into the back of the chair, instinctively putting distance between her baby and those probing eyes.

He blinked again and turned his attention back to something Doyle had said. Freed from the mesmerizing spell, Jolene expelled a sigh of unexpected relief.

What the heck had just happened? She didn't think Kellison had been scoping her out as a pretty woman or potential conquest. He was judging her for some reason. Judging her and deciding she'd come up short, even though they'd done nothing more than exchange names.

And some seriously intense eye contact.

With a grunt of exasperation, she turned and tossed her empty milk carton into the trash. Nate Kellison's I'm-here-to-work-not-make-friends attitude pricked at her sense of fair play, that was all. When she looked through the window again, he was following Doyle out the back hallway to the three bays where the Turning Point ambulance and engines were parked.

"The view's better from this side, buddy," she muttered as he turned his back to her. It was a silly, defensive retort, but one she realized was halfway true.

Without the intensity of those amber eyes to make her feel like a specimen beneath a microscope, she could relax and enjoy the scenery. From this vantage point, she could almost envision the laid-back surfer dude she'd expected to meet and share a few laughs with. Almost.

Laid-back didn't fit Nate Kellison. Not in any way, shape or form. Like his sparsity of words, there was something tightly controlled about the way he moved. His dark blue shirt clung to the rolling flex of his shoulders and his tapering back. Even lower, his glutes bunched and released beneath the drape of his uniform slacks, creating a taut, lean silhouette.

But something was off.

Before he disappeared around the corner, she lowered her gaze past the squared-off hips, the powerful thighs, and spied a subtle unevenness to his gait. The glitch in his body's disciplined perfection was nearly undetectable. But it was there.

Surprising.

Curious.

All that muscle and control, and the man walked with a limp.

Wounded.

"Oh, no." That chink in his armor humanized him. Stoic and grumpy she could handle. She could even get used to those all-seeing eyes. She could ignore his perfect tush and forgive his California roots.

But if he was in pain, she was in trouble.

Stray puppy syndrome, her father called it. Orphaned pets. Abandoned fathers. Wounded men. She was a sucker for them every damn time.

Jolene clenched her fists as the familiar emotion sparked inside her. *No,* she warned herself. *Don't do it.* But despite his less than friendly response to her, Nate Kellison's secrets were already tugging at more than her curiosity. How had he hurt himself? When did it happen? Was he in pain right now?

Thankfully a loud eruption of male laughter diverted her attention and gave her an excuse to squelch that dangerous rise of compassion.

Jolene shifted her focus, grateful for the distraction. Micky Flynn, the tall, flirtatious pilot, doffed her a salute and a handsome smile. Grinning, Jolene waved in return and watched him turn back to the new female volunteers. Unlike the ultra-intense Kellison, Micky was easy for most women to lust after. With his handsome face and daredevil personality, he was a natural-born lady-killer. But Micky and Jolene had never been more than friends. Maybe that was because she was the boss's daughter, a co-worker. Or maybe she was just too tied to the land to have much in common with a man who loved the sky.

She was all about home. Stability. Community. Taking care of her ranch. Taking care of her friends. Taking care of her family.

No matter how small that family might be.

Jolene flattened her hand against the blossoming curve of her belly and tried to picture the precious little boy growing inside her. Joaquin Angel, Jr., was a tiny miracle of modern science and answered prayers.

The science hadn't saved her husband, and the prayers had changed over the past few months. But she loved her little guy. He was hers alone now. And she cherished pending motherhood in a way her own mother never had.

One of those tender, butterfly flutters stirred beneath the press of her hand. At five months, he was still too small to deliver a real kick, but she could feel him shift inside her. An intuitive connection bonded them already. He'd know what it was like to grow up with only one parent, the way she had. He'd also know what it was like to have that one parent love him more than life itself.

The way she had.

Little Joaquin would never be abandoned. Not by

choice. Not by fate. "I'll always be here for you, sweetie," she crooned, stroking her belly as if she could caress the baby himself. "Grandpa, too."

Jolene looked up, intent on finding her father, to tell him she loved him with one of their coded winks.

Though he was engaged in a conversation with Dr. Sherwood, he winked right back and she smiled. His steady reassurance grounded her in a way that nothing else ever had. She was proud of him. Still handsome at fifty with those piercing blue eyes and easy smile, he had a friendly confidence about him that commanded respect, as evidenced by the way Dr. Sherwood nodded her head, then quickly crossed to the supply shelves to do his bidding.

Her father pointed to Jolene and then the outside door, marching his fingers through the air in imitation of someone walking. Subtle hint. Not.

Jolene shook her head and mouthed, *"No way."*

He shrugged and moved to the podium at the end of the room, where he picked up the latest printout from the weather bureau. He was such a worrier. A frown creased his brow as he pored over the stats, and she wished there wasn't a crowd or phone lines to monitor so she could run in and give him a hug.

Jolene knew her father carried the same sadness inside him that she did. A part of him would always love the beautiful woman who'd left them twenty years ago for the bright lights of Hollywood. Of course, April Kannon had never become a star like the L.A. talent agent she'd left with had promised. But she'd found two more husbands willing to provide her with the glitz and glamour and excitement she'd never found in tiny, remote Turning Point.

Mitch Kannon had been a rock when Jolene's mother had abandoned them. He'd been there for Jolene's first period, her first driving lesson, her first broken heart when she'd realized boys didn't date plain, skinny girls who could outrun and outride them.

He'd held her when she announced she was marrying her best friend—when she told him Joaquin was dying of cancer and that she'd agreed to be artificially inseminated with his sperm to create a child whose bone marrow could save his life. Her father was by her side the day Joaquin lost his battle with cancer, the morning she buried him.

How could she not be here for him now that he needed her?

"Ladies and gentlemen." Mitch Kannon's booming bass voice rattled the glass. He rapped his knuckles against the podium to get everyone's attention. "If we could get started. It's already a few minutes past eight, and I have a feeling we're going to have a long day. First, I want to brief you on the current weather forecast. Then we'll review procedure, what we can and should expect as far as casualties, and then I'll get you to your assignments."

Nate Kellison reentered with Doyle Brown, but hung back, opting to perch on the corner of a counter near the back of the room while Doyle took a seat in a chair closer to the podium.

There Nate sat, watching again. Friendly enough to get the job done, but not Texas friendly.

"What's your story, California?" Jolene whispered the rhetorical words to the glass.

What was he doing? Evaluating the acoustics of the

room? Looking for a chair beside a pretty woman he *could* get friendly with? She wondered if it was arrogance or professionalism or something more personal that pushed him to maintain such control over himself and the space around him.

The ringing of the telephone cut short her speculation about the visiting paramedic, and she turned to take the call. It wasn't a 9-1-1 call through the radio or emergency line. That probably meant it was another lost evacuee.

Jolene snapped up the receiver and grabbed her notepad. "Turning Point Fire Station. This is Jolene. How can I help you?"

"Jolene? Thank God. It's me—" The sharp catch of a familiar voice, followed by a low-pitched moan, put Jolene on immediate alert.

"Lily? Are you all right?" Jolene checked her watch and jotted down the time. The moan ended with a series of shallow, repetitive breaths. She didn't need a medical degree to figure out why her friend Lily Browning had called. Nine months pregnant and due any day, the woman had gone into labor. "Where are you?"

"I'm at home." Home was the Rock-a-Bye Ranch, just a few miles down the road from the Double J spread Jolene had inherited from Joaquin. "If this is what I think it is, I'm about a week early."

Lily sounded remarkably calm, now that the contraction had passed, giving Jolene a chance to hear the whoop of one of the three Browning boys hollering in the background. Jolene cupped her own belly and grinned, sending up a prayer that her son would be every bit as healthy and happy as Lily's were.

But she knew her neighbor hadn't called to share the joys and frustrations of motherhood the way they had so many mornings over herbal tea in one kitchen or the other. Jolene pushed to her feet, shedding her wistful thoughts and becoming the professional caretaker she needed to be. "With Doc Holland gone, the clinic's still closed. You'll have to get Gabe to drive you over to the Kingsville hospital. I'll call ahead and tell them to expect you."

But this wasn't going to be as easy as a phone call.

"Gabe isn't here. He had to go out of town on business. He must have gotten caught in the evac traffic. He was driving back through Dallas to get my mom to come help watch the kids when the baby comes." A shout for *"Mom!"* and a stampede of little feet crescendoed in the background. A rustling sound muffled Lily's stern warning.

"Aaron! Quit chasing Seth. If you want to run around, go outside."

"But it's raining."

"It's warm enough. Go get wet."

A chorus of *"woo-hoo's"* and various dibs were punctuated by the slamming of a door. Lily's home echoed with an ominous silence.

Jolene frowned at what that silence meant. "Are you there by yourself?"

"Just me and the boys." Lily's oldest was only going into the third grade. Not much help there. "Rocky got out through a downed fence, so I sent Deacon to retrieve him in case the storm blows this way."

The Brownings' live-in ranch hand had a hard enough time corraling their stubborn Santa Gertrudis bull when the weather was nice. Rocky had no concept of the phrase, *when the cows come home,* and seemed to think fences and ropes and rules were for inferior beings like heifers and cowboys. Add rain, mud and a possible hurricane to complicate things, and Rocky would probably keep Deacon away from the house for the rest of the day.

Jolene turned around, trying to get her father's attention. But he was pointing to a county map on the wall and had his back to her.

"How far apart are your contractions?" she asked, drumming her fingers against the glass window. Adrenaline poured into her veins, charging her body with a restless energy.

"I'm not sure. Fifteen minutes, maybe."

Jolene hadn't gotten her father's attention, but she was suddenly aware of someone else's probing stare focused on her. Her breath caught in her chest as she met Nate Kellison's golden brown gaze. His expression could be curiosity, could be concern. Could be contempt, for all she knew. Whatever it was, he seemed to look straight beyond any physical barriers and read what was in her mind and heart.

Her cheeks and other parts of her anatomy suffused with a heat that wasn't entirely due to self-conscious awareness. Her response was completely unexpected and too damn distracting to deal with at the moment. Needing to concentrate, Jolene quickly turned and showed him her backside.

"Do you have a watch, Lily?" Jolene fought to stay focused on the call. "You need to be sure."

Hell. If she could read a man's moods, maybe she'd

have found one of her own and fallen in love by now instead of ruling southeast Texas as every man's best buddy or kid sister. Joaquin didn't count. She'd been able to read her husband like a book. Of course, there'd never been any real passion between them to muddy up her perception, either.

Not that she was feeling passion toward Nate Kellison. No, sir. That tingling sense of hyper-awareness could be attributed to any number of things.

Like annoyance. Irritation.

Fascination. He was wounded, after all.

Oh, hell.

Fortunately, her personal life wasn't the issue right now. Ignoring the sensation of whiskey-brown eyes searing holes into her back, she went through the mental checklist of questions she should ask in this type of emergency. "Did your water break?"

"No. But after three kids, I know a contraction when I feel one." Lily exhaled a deep, stuttering breath. For the first time, Jolene heard the hint of fear in her friend's voice. "The baby's coming early. And I think she's coming fast."

Jolene checked her watch. Eight-fifteen. The Rock-a-Bye Ranch was a good twenty to thirty minute drive from town. "What do you mean by *fast?* You know that labors tend to be shorter with successive pregnancies."

"I guess I mean unexpected. This hit me all of the sudden this morning while I was fixing breakfast. Just before the rain started. With the boys, I had a real urge to cook and clean two or three days before they were born. But not this time. I haven't got a single casserole in the freezer, and this place is a mess." Lily tried to sound hopeful, while Jolene's concern mounted. "That means she's a girl, right?"

Because the nesting instinct hadn't kicked in yet? "Um, I can't tell you that, Lily. What about the radio? Can you call Deacon back to the house to drive you in?"

"That old coot? Deacon keeps the radio turned off because he says it spooks his horse. Unless he calls in again, I won't hear—"

A low-pitched moan. Another contraction. Jolene checked her watch and her notes and heaved a worried sigh. "Ho, boy."

Lily's fifteen minutes plus the five they'd been talking made her contractions just twenty minutes apart.

"This just feels different, Jolene." Lily was practicing her Lamaze breathing again. "You know how badly Gabe and I want a girl. We'd be happy with another boy, too. I just want him or her to be healthy. But to be honest, I'm a little worried. The timing feels off."

Off was not good. Alone at the ranch, twenty minutes from the nearest help, was definitely not good.

Jolene started to pace. "Lily, put your boys in the car and come into town. Especially if you think something's wrong. We've got staff on hand at the fire station who can monitor the baby's progress and help deliver her."

"I'm not sure that's a good idea. Deacon's last transmission was from down by the highway. He said the traffic's already lining up into town, that Sheriff Boone's out there trying to make sense of things and get the cars moving. What if we get stuck?"

"Take the backroads, then. You know the way."

"I guess I could do that."

Jolene's own stomach constricted in sympathy as Lily caught a sharp breath. "Lily?"

"Don't worry. That wasn't a contraction." A pain that wasn't a contraction was supposed to reassure her? "Maybe we could get there before the rains make a mess of those old gravel roads." Lily covered up the phone and hollered, "Boys!"

A sudden image of Lily's old station wagon, mired axle-deep in the mud, flashed through Jolene's mind. Gabe had no doubt taken their newer, more reliable vehicle to Dallas to pick up Lily's mother. Three boys—two, five and eight—buckled into a rattletrap car, their pregnant mother in labor in the front seat. Rains and wind and flooding on the way, maybe even the hurricane itself.

Not good at all.

Decision made, Jolene stopped in her tracks, her resolve as determined as her posture. "On second thought, stay put. I'm coming to you."

Was that audible sigh one of relief?

Jolene quickly scratched a note for her father. "You sit tight, Lily. Make yourself as comfortable as you can and give the boys something to keep them busy. I'll grab a med kit and head on out to the Rock-A-Bye right now."

"Are you sure?"

"Hey. This is what I do. We're neighbors. We're friends. I know somethin' about birthin' babies and I'm on my way."

Lily laughed at the dubious reference to *Gone with the Wind*. "Okay. Thanks."

"Hey, now don't you go chasing any cattle yourself, okay?"

"Promise. We'll sit tight until you get here."

Jolene hung up the phone, tore off the note and hurried out of the office. With her father in the middle of outlining the county's layout and evacuation routes, and everyone listening with dutiful attention, Jolene dashed across the back of the room to the supply shelves.

She picked up one of the portable paramedic kits, knowing that between it, the emergency supplies in her truck, and whatever the Brownings had on hand at the house, she'd have everything she'd need to deliver Lily's baby if there wasn't enough time to get her friend back into town. She silently snapped her fingers in a moment of inspiration and hurried over to the wall of cabinets.

She opened the first one and scanned the contents. *Nope.* Moving on to the next cabinet, she spotted the goodies she'd stashed away. She set the med kit on the counter and stretched up on tiptoe to grasp the prize she was looking for. A bag of chocolate candy left over from Easter. She might snitch one to satisfy her own cravings, but she could use them as a reward for the Browning boys in case she had to take care of them as well as Lily.

Jolene jumped in her boots as she closed the cabinet door and a broad set of blue-clad shoulders came into view.

"Problem?"

Pressing her hand to her chest to soothe the startled leap in her heart rate, Jolene looked up past the jut of Nate Kellison's chin and straight into those omniscient brown eyes. "Nothing that concerns you, California."

"Nate."

"Right." She tucked the bag of candy into the pocket of her overalls and reached for the handle of the med kit.

Before she could leave, his hand settled over hers, pushing the kit back onto the counter. "You're not going out on a call, are you?"

His grip was firm, warm—and sent a crazy little frisson of electricity up her arm. His succinct query rolled across her eardrums in a deep-pitched whisper. Dormant emotions awakened inside her at the surprising intimacies of sound and touch, emotions that were all too vulnerable and uniquely feminine. Emotions she quickly shut down by breaking the connection. She slid her hand from beneath his, willing the tingling sensation of his callused fingertips brushing across her skin to dissipate.

In one practiced, self-conscious motion, she tucked a loose strand of hair behind her ear and pointed toward her father, avoiding those eyes that seemed to possess the power to read her silly reaction to his touch. "You're missing the briefing."

The slight turn of his head was all the diversion she needed to grab the med kit without answering his question. But their movements were enough to capture her father's attention as well. Jolene waved the note at him, indicating she'd leave it in the office. Then she turned her back on Nate Kellison and tried to sneak out without disturbing the rest of the meeting.

No such luck.

"Excuse me a minute." Jolene halted at the sound of her father's voice following her down the hallway. "Since you picked up a kit, I can guess that you're not going home?"

"I didn't mean to interrupt you," she apologized. To her chagrin, Kellison had followed her to the door as well. Setting her shoulders, she purposely ignored him standing behind her father. "Lily Browning called. She's gone into labor, but she's stranded at the ranch. I'm going to drive out to do what I can to help. If there's time, I'll drive her and the boys into town. If not, I'll deliver the baby there." She squeezed her father's arm reassuringly. "It won't be my first delivery."

Mitch Kannon nodded, his tone as businesslike as hers had been. "Give me ten minutes to finish this meeting, and I'll go with you."

She gestured down the hall. "You can't leave these people right now. You've got four virtual strangers who'll be lost in a minute without your directions, and a handful of locals who are half-distracted worrying about their own families and homes. They're looking to you for leadership. You have to stay with the command center."

"Nice speech," drawled Mitch. "But I still don't want you driving that far out into the county by yourself. The weather's unpredictable right now, and you're not exactly in the best condition to go gallivanting across the countryside."

"Dad! My *condition* doesn't make me stupid." Jolene didn't know whether to smile or frown at his flare of old-fashioned chauvinism. Opting for her most indulgent smile, she cradled the curve of her belly. "We're in perfect health. I'm done with morning sickness and nap attacks. The pregnancy is progressing fine. Nothing's going to happen to me or Junior just riding in the truck."

He shook his head. "You and I both know that's not the problem. With you, it's never just a *ride in the truck*."

"Lily's waiting, Dad."

"Can I help?" Mr. California wasn't content just observing her business, he had to butt in.

Bristling at the intrusion, she glanced over her father's shoulder. "No."

But Mitch angled himself to include Kellison in the discussion, ignoring her dismissal. "A friend of Jolene's is stuck out at her ranch. Just went into labor with her fourth baby."

"Fourth?" Kellison's eyebrows rose. "The baby could come fast, then. Within a few hours."

Jolene backed toward the door. "Exactly. I'd better get going."

Mitch stopped her. "Honey, why don't you stay and man the phones until Ruth gets here."

"Dad—"

"I'll go." Kellison's statement was directed at Mitch. "I've been trained to deliver babies under a variety of conditions." He pointed his thumb over his shoulder. "You'll need Cheryl and Amy here to handle the more serious patients as they come in. Your daughter can stay in the office."

Of all the annoying, arrogant... Jolene planted her empty hand on her hip and squared off against the visiting paramedic. "Do you know the way to the Rock-a-Bye Ranch, California?"

"It's Nate." He turned to her father. "You got a map?"

"*I* know the way," she insisted. "We're wasting time discussing this."

Oh, no. She could read the decision on her father's face.

"You're right about needing the doctor and trauma nurse here," Mitch said. "You go with her, Kellison."

"Dad—"

"He's a trained paramedic."

"Which is why you need him here," she argued. "For real emergencies. I can handle this and be back in no time."

"Listen, young lady. What I need right now is to not worry about you or Lily Browning. Kellison goes with you, or you stay put."

Father and daughter glared at each other. But the silent battle of wills didn't last for long. Once Mitch Kannon dug in his heels, he couldn't be budged. And as much as she loathed the idea of being assigned a babysitter while she made a routine call at a friend's house, Jolene didn't want to cause her father any additional worry when she knew he had a whole county and hundreds of additional evacuees to protect.

"All right." Watching the worry ease from her father's expression made agreeing more tolerable.

He hugged her and kissed her goodbye. "Be sure to call in and keep me posted."

"I will. Love you."

He winked. "Love you." Then he released her and grasped Kellison's shoulder. "You've got the most important job in the county, as far as I'm concerned. Keep my little girl safe."

"Dad—"

"Yes, sir."

"Chief?" Doyle Brown called from the end of the hallway. He pointed to his watch. "You said to keep an eye on the time?"

"Let me know if Lily finally gets her girl," Mitch ordered over his shoulder as he hurried back to the main room. The phone rang in the dispatch office as he passed by. "And so it begins," he muttered, just loud enough for

Jolene to hear. "Doyle! Come answer this phone." She watched her father disappear around the corner and take command of his audience once more. "All right, boys and girls, let's get down to business…"

Nate Kellison pulled a blue ball cap from his back pocket and slipped it into place over his head. The letters CBFD, embroidered in white, stood out in sharp contrast against the dark material. Neat and tidy and in control. *Lordy.* Wasn't this going to be fun?

His fingers brushed against her arm. "Shall we?"

Feeling betrayed by the heat that rushed to her elbow in response to his touch, Jolene headed toward the door. But she didn't get a chance to escape.

Kellison pried the med kit from her hand and reached around her to open the door. Jolene spun around, narrowly avoiding bumping into his chest. "I'm not an invalid. I can take—"

Her words stopped as abruptly as she had. He wasn't an extraordinarily tall man, maybe six feet, like her father. But up close like this, with her eyes mere centimeters from his chin, his arm circling around her without quite touching her, he seemed much bigger, stronger than his lean build would indicate. Her pulse tripped a beat. She stood close enough that her nose could detect he wore no cologne, no aftershave. But the clean, distinct smells of soap and man addled her thinking long enough that she didn't finish her sentence.

"I'm sure you can," he answered for her. "I'm just following your father's orders."

Her gaze was automatically drawn to the tense line of his lips, which softened as he spoke. But the air outside the open door gusted, blowing a fine mist against her skin. The chilly dampness took the edge off her indignant temper and cooled the sensation of heat radiating from his body into hers.

Jolene backed up a step and tilted her chin. "Why don't you like me, Mr. Kellison?"

She reached out to retrieve the med kit, but his grip tightened around the handle and wouldn't budge. "I don't know whether I like you or not, Jolene. I don't even know you."

She pulled her hand away and crossed her arms. "And yet you keep looking at me with the judgment of Solomon in your eyes."

"Do I?"

"Yes. And it's very disconcerting."

"Then I'll quit looking." Jolene's heart raced as he stared at her for an endless moment, searching her face as if—as he'd promised—this was to be his last look and he wanted to remember every ordinary detail.

Finally the scrutiny was too much and she lowered her gaze to the triangle of white cotton T-shirt that showed beneath the unbuttoned collar of his uniform. "Mr. Kellison. You're staring again."

She was suddenly aware that her lip gloss had gone the way of her roll and milk. She hadn't taken the time to put on any other makeup that might give her some semblance of feminine beauty. The maternity overalls she hadn't fully grown into hung like a sack from her shoulders, hiding what little figure she did have.

Still, the intensity of his look made her think he saw something else in her. Something that made her wish…

Jolene started as he tapped the point of her chin with one blunt fingertip and urged her gaze back up to his.

But there was nothing romantic or even reassuring in the familiar gesture. He just wanted her attention.

"My mistake," he said, his voice devoid of emotion. "I'll haul. You drive."

The imprint of his touch remained when he pulled away. He glanced over his shoulder as he turned and strode out into the rain. "And it's Nate."

CHAPTER THREE

THE JUDGMENT OF SOLOMON?

Hell. Just what had he revealed in his unabashed study of Jolene Kannon-Angel? Those true blue eyes of hers were pretty hard to ignore, especially when they were focused his way. Nate thought he'd sensed trouble, and his instinct had been to find the source, to do what he could to help.

And then...well hell, even when she turned on that attitude, it was hard to look away. He'd dated prettier women, made friends with decidedly less-complicated ones. But Jolene...?

Instincts of self-preservation told him to walk a wide berth around her smart mouth and pregnant belly. But something else—maybe the old soul inside him that had seen too much pain and death in twenty-nine years—warned him to stick close and do whatever he could to keep her and her baby out of trouble.

Why don't you like me?

He honestly couldn't say whether he liked her or not. They'd known each other for barely more than an hour.

He hated the distance she insisted on putting between them—defiant glares, refusing to call him by his given name. He wondered what the heck she had against the people of California.

There were things he did like about her. He liked the color of her eyes, liked discovering that her skin felt every bit as smooth and creamy as it looked. He liked watching her soft pink lips move when she talked—and she talked a lot. He liked that she was so loyal to her father and hometown.

But he thought Texans were pretty damn foolish to let their pregnant women work in dangerous situations. Yeah, they were shorthanded in Turning Point, and could use all the help they could get. But if that help was a headstrong female like the willowy blond driver sitting across the truck from him, barreling over the rutted gravel roads west of town as if she was trying to lap the competition in a road rally, then he definitely had a problem with how they handled things down here in Texas.

That's what he didn't like.

Solomon would surely agree.

Nate bounced off his seat at the next bump, then came back down, relaxing his posture to absorb the jolt. He'd had smoother rides on the back of a bull during his competition days. He adjusted the shoulder strap of his seat belt and let his gaze slide across the truck's tweedy upholstery to double-check for the umpteenth time that Jolene was wearing hers as well.

Deliver a baby? Right. They'd be damn lucky if they reached the Rock-a-Bye Ranch without having to radio in for a tow truck or ambulance themselves.

Crazy Texas woman.

She could learn a thing or two about patience and wisdom from Solomon.

"Are we trying to set a new record?" he ventured to ask. "Cross-country racing at warp speeds? Testing how long it takes to completely destroy the undercarriage on your truck?"

"Ha. Ha. So you *do* have a sense of humor." Her long ponytail bobbed across her shoulders as she darted a look at him. "Too bad it's not an amusing one."

"Eyes on the road, Andretti."

She faced forward. "It's *Jolene*."

"Ha. Ha." He took the verbal payback like a big boy. But her speed did slow a fraction.

If he used his imagination.

He kept his hand braced on the armrest, but settled back into his seat to ride this out. The rain was picking up in intensity, cutting down visibility with every milepost they passed. It wasn't a full-blown storm yet—the drops still fell in straight sheets and the clouds hadn't charged enough to create visible lightning. But judging by the gray-green squall line he could see closing in behind them in the sideview mirror, it was only a matter of time before something truly serious hit.

Maybe Mitch Kannon's internal radar was right. Hurricane Damon might be turning.

All the more reason to pick up Mrs. Browning and her boys and get them and Jolene back to safety at the evac shelter.

With the brim of his cap shading his eyes, Nate glanced over to study the determined set of Jolene's profile. "You know, you won't save anybody if we don't get to the ranch in one piece."

Her sleek shoulders stiffened, no doubt taking the gentle suggestion as criticism. "You heard what Sheriff Boone said on the radio. The highway is backed up halfway to Chapman Ranch. They're going to start rerouting folks through Bishop, and then both of the main roads into town will be slow. I'd like to get Lily and her boys to the high school, where someone can help take care of them after the baby arrives. I do *not* want to be stuck in traffic. I hate sitting still when I know there's something I could be doing to help."

Nate almost smiled at the blatantly obvious statement. "So I gathered."

She shot him a look—either admiring his dry wit, or wishing he'd fly out the window at the next bump.

She nearly got her wish.

The truck lurched on its chassis as if she'd slammed on the brakes. "Son of a—"

"Jolene!"

But her foot was still on the accelerator. She whipped her focus back to the road as they plowed through a sluggish patch of newly formed mud.

"Damn!"

"Look out!" Instinctively Nate's hand snaked out to grab her shoulder and steady her. His bum knee thumped against the dashboard, but the sharp shot of pain that radiated through the joint was nothing compared with the heart-stopping images of certain tragedy that flashed through his brain.

Mangled truck.

Pregnant woman screaming in pain.

Dead baby.

"Ah, hell." Nate blanked his mind to the past and future and concentrated on the here and now. Three thin lines, marking a barbed-wired fence, loomed into view and he braced for impact. "Turn it!"

"I am!"

Nate grabbed the wheel between her white-knuckled fists and jerked it to the right, matching the tires to the skid. As soon as they hit solid brush and harder ground, they spun left.

Jolene's shoulder bumped his chest; their heads nearly smacked. But together they regained control of the fishtailing vehicle and steered their course back between the ditches. Muddy water sprayed up onto the windshield, blanketing their view for a split second before the wipers cleared a visual path. Gravel ricocheted beneath the floorboards.

They bumped over ruts and flattened them, created new ones in the soupy sandtrap of parched dirt that had soaked up too much rain. But they were slowing. Gaining traction. Going straight. In control once more.

Jolene tapped the brake and finally brought the truck to a stop in the middle of the road. "Ooh!" She ground the gear into Park, pounded the wheel with her fist, then sat up straight in her seat.

Nate released the wheel and slowly leaned back, keeping his hand on her quaking shoulder, just in case something more than temper or panic had put the splotches of color in her cheeks. "You okay?" he asked.

Her chest rose and fell in quick, deep gasps. But with a jerky determination, she smoothed a long strand of hair behind her ear and nodded. She darted him a sideways glance of clear true blue. Another good sign. "You?"

"I'm fine." His knee twinged, making a liar out of him. But he ignored it. "The baby?"

She shrugged her shoulder from his grasp. "He's fine, too."

Stubborn woman. Would it kill her to accept him as an ally? At least in the taking-care-of-people department?

Nate's breath eased out on a weary sigh. When he inhaled again, he breathed in the home-baked smells that clung to Jolene's hair and clothes. Simple. Clean. Wholesome. It was a bit of a challenge for his jaded frame of mind to be this close and maintain his annoyance with her reckless behavior. He untwisted his seat belt and sank back onto his side of the cab. "Should I even ask about the truck?"

With the efficiency of a cockpit crew, she checked the buttons and dials on the dashboard, shifted the truck into Drive and tried to straighten the steering wheel. "It feels like I've screwed up the alignment. Damn, damn, damn!" she muttered on three different pitches. Her burst of temper dissipated on a soft breath. "Sorry. You didn't hear that."

"Don't apologize…"

Nate's voice trailed off when he realized she wasn't excusing her frustrated curse to him. Her head bowed and she slid her left hand down to gently rub her belly. She was apologizing to the baby.

As he listened to her coo maternal words to the life growing inside her, something tender and slightly awestruck curled inside him, soothing the frayed remnants of his concern like the steady drumbeat of rain against the roof of the truck. Protective feelings were nothing new to him. He'd long been his sister's staunchest supporter, as well as big brother to a dozen other female friends over the years, because listening and watching and fixing problems came easily to an old soul like him.

Only, he wasn't feeling quite so patient or wise around Jolene Kannon-Angel. Despite her tough talk and tomboyish exterior, there was something utterly feminine about her sweet nurturing instincts, something more vulnerable than foolish about the risks she was willing to take for others—something that spoke to him.

But he couldn't say he was feeling brotherly toward her. He felt compassion, sure. Frustration, definitely. There was even that buzz of hyper-awareness that had awakened inside him at his first glimpse of those incredible blue eyes.

Nope. Judging by the way his temper simmered in his veins each time she took an unnecessary risk, the way her eclectic behavior baffled, yet intrigued him, the way her soft skin and megawatt smile kindled a noticeable response due south of his belt buckle, *brotherly* didn't even make the list.

Of course, he shouldn't be sitting here, stuck halfway to nowhere on this backwater road, having any feelings whatsoever. Jolene was recently widowed. There was a woman in labor anxiously awaiting their arrival. They'd nearly wrecked the truck and, oh yeah, there was a hurricane on the way.

Work. Gotta work.

"Should we get moving again?" he prompted, needing to get his mind focused on the task at hand before he did something stupid like reach over to brush aside that wayward strand of hair that had fallen across her forehead and cheek again. He tapped his watch instead. "If you're in one piece, we should go."

She quickly placed both hands on the wheel and nodded. If her sigh was any indication, he'd done an effective job of spoiling the quiet mood and getting them back on track. He should be feeling a little more satisfaction, rather than swallowing down the regret that seemed to catch in his throat.

She slid her gaze in his direction without making eye contact. "You sure you're okay? You keep rubbing that knee."

Nate's hand stilled on his right thigh. He hadn't been aware that he'd started the massage that occasionally brought him relief on days when his leg was giving him fits. But Jolene had noticed.

Her blue eyes had connected with his now, and the blend of curiosity and compassion he saw there was as unsettling as the realization that she'd noticed his pain even when he refused to. He was the caretaker here. He'd promised her father he'd watch out for *her*. Not the other way around.

He patted his leg, making light of her concern. "It's an old injury from college. It acts up whenever the barometric pressure drops. Like today."

His explanation wasn't convincing anybody.

Especially Jolene. "Is that why you limp? Are you in pain all the time?"

She'd noticed that, too?

Nate stared at her in disbelief, his teeth clenched so tight he could feel his pulse ticking along his jaw. Hell. He must have left his cool, calm and collected pill back in California. Maybe on the side of the highway with that baby he couldn't save. Maybe back home on the ranch where he no longer felt at home.

This crazy Texas woman with the barbed tongue and the beautiful eyes confounded him at every turn. He was

reacting to things she said and did, instead of staying in
control of his emotions and on task. He had to get a grip
on whatever it was he was trying to feel, or he wasn't
going to be much good as a volunteer to Mitch or Turning Point or anybody else.

"Yeah, it's a permanent handicap," he finally admitted.

The doctors had stitched up all the parts they could
find. They'd added a few made of plastic and steel. Still,
one leg would always be shorter than the other. One
knee would never flex like the other. It would stop him
at airport gates and keep him off the dance floor for anything faster than a waltz. It would be a target for arthri-
tis before his time.

But he always played the injury down so nobody
would notice. So nobody would treat him differently. So
no one would think him any less capable, any less a man.

But Jolene noticed. "I didn't think you were handicapped. I just thought you'd hurt yourself surfing or ski-
ing or whatever it is you do out in California. Did I make
it worse? You should have said something. I can drive
slow if you need me to."

"What?" Just what kind of old fart did she think he
was, anyway? "*You* need to slow down—" *Your entire
life,* Nate wanted to add. *To keep that baby and your own
skin safe.* But caught himself before his temper flared.
Using that betraying right hand to remove his cap, he
smoothed his hair and adjusted the hat back into place—
adjusting his focus at the same time. "Look, I'm fine,"
he reassured her, forcing half a grin to appear more convincing. "This leg isn't any worse off than it was before.
Lily Browning's the one I'm worried about."

Apparently he was convincing enough to alleviate

her concern and get her focused on something besides his shortcomings. Good.

"Me, too." Jolene shifted the truck into drive. "I mean, Dad would have called us with an update if there was any change in Lily's condition. But we should still get there as soon as we can."

"Agreed." Nate stared out the window. The sky was turning grayer by the minute.

"And we won't tell Dad about banging up my truck, okay? Since neither of us was hurt, and the truck still runs, I don't see any need to report it. He'll find out soon enough, and he worries about me too much as it is."

Was it any wonder? But Nate nodded his agreement. Mitch had more than enough to handle today. Keeping Jolene out of trouble might be the best thing he could do to help her father. "That's your call."

"Yes, it is." He glanced over at the sharp tone in her voice. But he suspected it had more to do with the worsening weather conditions than with him. The quick smile she spared him went a long way toward lightening his mood. "But thanks, anyway."

He supposed keeping a secret was one small thing she'd let him do for her. "No problem."

Jolene flipped the windshield wipers up to high and pressed on the accelerator, taking them along the soggy road at a saner speed. Though he could tell she was concentrating hard to steer the misaligned truck over the challenging terrain, nothing seemed able to stop her mouth. "I'm sorry if I hit a nerve," she apologized. "I mean that figuratively, not literally. Unless I did hit a nerve, and that's why your knee hurts—"

"Just drive."

They jostled along for another half mile. "So what was it?" she asked.

"What was what?" Man, she liked to talk. About as fast as she liked to drive.

"What happened to your leg? You don't look big enough for football. Was it a surfing accident? Skateboarding? Tripping over a star in Hollywood?"

Actually it had been one son of a bitch bull that hadn't taken a shine to rodeo life, being ridden, or Nate. Tossing his rider to the ground before his eight seconds were up hadn't been enough payback. And though Nate's memories were a little fuzzy after seeing a thousand plus pounds of angry bull charging him, when he woke up in the ambulance, he'd been quite clear about the fact his college rodeo scholarship and planned career as a professional bull rider were over.

Hollywood star? Yeah, right. "You've got some serious misconceptions about California."

"I know all I need to about the Golden State." Now there was a cryptic statement. "So what about your leg?"

They bounced over to the left side of the road to avoid a pool of water standing in a washout. As they eased back over the stubby weeds in the middle, he caught a glimpse of something cream-colored dashing into the road.

The inquisition was forgotten. Nate grabbed the dash and leaned forward. "What's that?"

"I see it."

Jolene slowed the truck. Despite the reflective wall of rain in front of them, she turned on the headlights to give them a better look.

Too big to be a coyote. Too small to be a horse. Dancing back and forth too quickly to be a vehicle of any kind.

Jolene slammed on the brakes the instant the object came into focus. "Oh, my God!"

"What the hell?"

Crazy Texans.

Arms waved as the figure jumped up and down, a long filmy cloth slapping against bare shoulders with every jump. Nate cracked open his window. He could hear the shouting now. A blonde woman in a wedding gown and veil was out in the middle of the road, flagging them down.

"Help! Stop! Please! Oh, thank God." She glanced over her shoulder toward a stand of tall, dead brown grass in the ditch behind her. "Wes!"

She looked barely old enough to have graduated from high school. The would-be, runaway—or on her way to a costume party—bride hiked up her limp skirt and dashed toward the truck.

Nate glanced across the seat as she approached. "A friend of yours?"

He was thinking along the lines of impulsive soul mate, but Jolene shook her head. "I don't recognize her. She's not from Turning Point."

The bedraggled bride ran straight for the driver's side of the vehicle. *Hell.* Instead of just rolling down her window to talk, Jolene was already climbing out. With a resolute sigh, Nate pulled his cap low on his forehead and opened his door.

"Hey, you okay?" Jolene squeezed the young woman's outstretched hand.

"I am now. Can you help us?" Though breathless with panic, the young woman didn't show any obvious signs of injury.

As Nate rounded the hood of the truck, it was impossible to tell if the streaks of mascara running down her face were from tears or the weather. But one thing was clear. Spots of rain had already dappled the back of Jolene's overalls. Another few minutes outside like this, and she'd be just as wet as the bride. He needed to assess the situation and get them out of there as quickly as possible.

"You guys lost?" he asked, including the equally young man in a mud-splattered tuxedo who was climbing out of the ditch to join them. The kid seemed to be moving fine, under his own power. He carried a tire iron.

Nate felt no threat, though. Without the glare from the windshield, he could get a look at the dinged-up compact turned sideways in the ditch, its front fender pointed up at the sky, its back tires mired in the mud. He could make out what was left of a skid trail, now a trough of mud and gravel.

A flat tire. A blowout, most likely. The kids were lucky they hadn't rolled the vehicle.

The bride jabbed a thumb over her shoulder at her groom. "Ask Wes. This was his idea of a shortcut."

"Now, Cindy, when you saw how backed-up the highway was, you agreed with me."

"I didn't agree to this!" Cindy crossed her arms and leaned toward Jolene, giving her a conspiratorial, only-a-woman-could-understand glare. "I'm supposed to be on my honeymoon in San Antonio right now."

The kid named Wes reached out to touch her. She stiffened and he pulled away. "C'mon, honey. I said I was—"

"Either of you two hurt?" Nate asked, cutting them off before the argument really got started.

Though the kid was caked in mud and streaked with grease, when Wes held out his hand, Nate took it. "No, sir, Officer. We popped a tire and ran off the road. I was just trying to change it."

He'd been trying for some time, by the look of things. Nate held on long enough to assess that the gold ring was real, and that the wrinkled, musky tux had been slept in or stayed up all night in even before he'd torn and stained it trying to fix the tire. These kids were newlyweds, all right, if not terribly bright ones.

Nate wiped his hand clean on the side of his leg. "First of all, I'm a paramedic, not a cop. You don't have to call me *sir.* Secondly, we're already on a call. If neither of you are seriously hurt, I suggest you wait in your car and we'll call a tow truck to come help you out ASAP."

"Sorry, sir. I mean…sorry." Wes's cheeks actually turned pink beneath the shaggy brown hair that mud and water had plastered to them.

"There's only one tow truck in Turning Point," Jolene informed him. "Riley Addams's rig. And he's one of the volunteer firefighters who works for Dad. Dad's going to want to keep him on hand in case there's a fire or injury emergency."

"What about the sheriff's department?"

Jolene shrugged. "You heard the dispatch. Most of them are busy directing traffic into town."

Nate propped his hands on his hips. *Just dandy.* More screwball Texas organization. But if these two were old enough to get married, then they were mature enough to accept some responsibility. He schooled his patience and offered a plausible alternative. "Maybe you could just sit tight, and we'll pick you up on the way back—after we check Mrs. Browning's condition."

"I'm not spending another minute with this twerp!" Cindy argued.

"Honey, you agreed with me this morning—"

"That was three hours ago." She whirled around and stamped her silver-sandaled foot in the mud. "Before the rain. Before my gown was ruined. Before your brother's stupid car fell apart on us."

"That wasn't my fault!"

She spun back to face Jolene and Nate. So much for maturity. "We've been planning this wedding for two months. You'd think he'd at least have the sense to make sure his own car was running."

"It *was* running last night."

"First, my beautiful sunrise wedding gets ruined by this stupid weather. Then the car doesn't work. And by the time we left Chapman Ranch, the highway was packed with people headed for Turning Point. So Wes took a detour. Now we're stuck. No hotel. No hot tub." She glared at her husband. "No honeymoon."

Wes looked embarrassed and exhausted. Not to mention drenched to the skin. "We don't have a cell phone or I would have called for help. We blew the right rear tire and spun out. I tried to fix it, but it's too muddy for the jack to work. We tried to drive out, but obviously, that didn't work, either."

Cindy was on a roll. "Obviously. If you'd listened to me, we'd—"

"Whoa, whoa, whoa." Nate held up his hands in a T

for time-out. "We're on an emergency call." But half of the *we* had already circled around the car to inspect the flat tire. "Jolene?" *Hell*. This just got better and better. Nate resisted the urge to shake his fist at these crazy fools. Somebody needed to be the sensible grown-up here. "I've got a woman in labor on the Rock-a-Bye ranch, so we can only spare a few minutes. If we can get you up and running in that time, we'll do it. If not, we call it in and you stay put until that tow truck can get here."

"But that could be—"

He cut off Cindy's whine in his most decisive, do-not-mess-with-me voice. "You go sit in the truck. Warm yourself up for a few minutes while I see what I can do. Wes, you're with me."

Cindy wanted to speak, but closed her mouth, wisely thinking better of it. With a huffy sigh, she marched around to open the truck's door while Wes shyly held out the tire iron. "You'll need this, sir."

"Don't call…" Oh, hell. Let the kid be a little intimidated. Maybe it'd knock some sense into him. Nate took the tire iron and winked a bit of reassurance. "Come on."

With the pouting bride safely tucked away inside the truck, Nate tipped his face to the sky, searching for a break among the clouds, challenging the warm rain to cleanse his skin and deeper inside. He needed to rid himself of his frustrations, stay calm and in charge.

Now he had more than Jolene and her baby to take care of.

Swiping the moisture from his face, Nate hiked around the car and found Jolene kneeling in the mud, her red boot already heel-deep in ditch water. She had her shoulder wedged up against the wheel well of the car as she tried to pry the jack free.

"Are you crazy?" Nate dashed the last few feet. He grabbed her by the upper arm and pulled her away from the potential danger. He raised his voice to be heard over the sound of raindrops slapping against the earth. "That whole thing could come crashing down on you. Get back in the truck. Wes and I will handle this."

Jolene jerked her arm from his grip, but not before his fingers memorized the sensations of delicate bone structure and sinewed muscle beneath her baggy sleeve. Not before his pulse leaped in response to the appealing combination of softness and strength.

"I know how to change a tire," she insisted, slicking her hair behind her ear and leaving a blemish of mud on her cheek. "The car's resting on the ground, not the jack. Once we get the jack unstuck, we could put some grass or gravel underneath it to keep it from sinking in again. Then we could lift the car, change the flat and get those two underway."

"That's your plan?" Actually it wasn't a half bad one, given the circumstances. Nate tamped down his sarcasm. Time was a factor, and Jolene's idea was as good as any. But he didn't want her messing with the tire. The danger of the car shifting might be minimal, but it was a danger, all the same.

"All right," he conceded. "Grab the hubcap while you're at it. We can use it under the jack to get firmer footing, too."

Hope or excitement or some other wonderful thing blazed in her eyes, making Nate feel like a prince for half a moment. Basking in the fleeting glory, he couldn't seem to stop himself from reaching out and flicking the smear of mud from her velvety cheek. A startled *oh* rounded her lips when he touched her, but she didn't pull away. Still, he didn't allow himself to linger. He was determined to be the prince of practicality. "I'll work on the tire. You gather whatever you can find to give us traction."

Jolene ran to the truck and came back with a hatchet and shovel. She handed the shovel to Wes and asked him to dig up gravel while she started hacking down handfuls of ground cover from either side of the ditch. Meanwhile, Nate flipped his cap around backward so the bill protected his neck, and he hunched down to inspect the tire for himself. The thing wasn't just flat; it was shredded.

Wes had loosened the bolts, but hadn't got much further. Ignoring the ache in his bum knee, Nate used the tire iron as a lever to free the jack from the mud. The next step was to lighten the back of the car.

Wading in up to his ankles, he took note that the water in the ditch was deep enough to form an eddy around his boots. The ground was too dry and hard to soak up the rain as quickly as it was falling. This had to be runoff from the flat cattle land. That meant the water would continue to rise—exponentially—in low-lying areas, even if the rain slowed or stopped, which Nate doubted was going to happen any time soon.

He had to work fast to get the honeymooners on their way. Faster, to pick up Lily Browning and get her back to Turning Point for the medical care she and her baby would need.

Nate hauled out two garment bags and a toiletry kit

from Wes and Cindy's trunk and carted them up to
the road.

"Those two don't believe in traveling light, do they,"
Jolene joked, cutting through a stubborn weed.

Nate set the items down beside her and headed back
to retrieve two large suitcases.

"Joaquin and I never had a honeymoon. He was already sick when we got married. He used to promise
that when—"

Her voice stopped abruptly and her wistful gaze
sharpened and darted up to Nate's, as if surprised that
she'd said the words out loud. Or maybe just surprised
that she'd said them to him.

He looked down at her over the corner of a suitcase.
That long strand of hair had worked loose from her ponytail again, and the rain had glued it to her face. "Joaquin was your husband, right?"

She nodded, but offered no more. She pushed to her
feet, carrying the pile of weeds with her. "I'll go see if
this is enough."

He watched her golden ponytail bob out of sight.
Taboo subject. Painful one, at least. In the few hours
he'd known her, it was the first thing that had come up
that she *wouldn't* talk about with him.

Which made Nate all the more curious. He wondered what kind of man Joaquin Angel had been. What
kind of man would Jolene love? How would she love?
Full speed ahead like everything else she did, no doubt.
Probably unlike any woman he'd ever known.

Of course, he'd never really been in love himself, so
he had nothing to compare. But he'd listened to enough
tales of passion rushing couples into mistakes they later

regretted. He'd nursed enough family and friends through their heartaches. He had no interest in Lady Disaster.

None whatsoever.

So why was he still standing here, soaking up the rain, trying to figure her out?

"Hell." Nate set down the suitcases and went back to work.

The rear end of the car teetered upward a couple of inches when he removed the last suitcase. He ignored Cindy's muffled cries and gesticulations from the cab of the truck. He was making some hard choices here. If she and Wes wanted to get to San Antonio, then their things were going to get wet.

But he couldn't ignore the water swirling past the top of his brown work boot and soaking the hem of his pantleg. "That's rising an inch a minute," he muttered, doing a quick calculation.

The clock was ticking way too fast.

Nate closed the trunk and climbed out of the ditch. Blinking the moisture from his eyelashes, he knelt beside Jolene, tugged the handle of the jack from her grasp and inserted it into the base. "Go back to the truck. I'll finish up here."

She tugged back. "I can do this."

He separated her hand from the jack and held on to both. "Go back to the truck and call this delay in to your father."

"*You* call it in."

"Damn it, lady, I'm not going to argue—" Temper gave way to a bone-deep awareness of danger gushing toward them.

"California?"

With only a splash of sound to alert him, the rear of the car rose and shifted toward them, carried on the current of water like a log on a flume. Time was up. "We're out of here."

With nearly a ton of metal sailing their way, Nate picked up Jolene, jack handle and all. He reached beneath her arm and cinched her between the swells of her breasts and belly. He ignored the protest of his knee and pushed to his feet, carrying her up to the center of the road.

"Put me down."

The instant she wiggled in protest, the instant the curve of her rump twisted against his crotch, the instant he realized she hid a distinctly feminine shape beneath her shapeless clothes, he set her on her feet. But he didn't trust her to keep moving. Switching his grip to her arm, he hurried her toward the truck.

"What are you doing?" she demanded, fighting him every step of the way. "The water's rising. We have to fix that car *now*."

Wes trailed after them, dragging the shovel and pointing to the floating car. "But my brother's—"

Nate didn't have time to argue with either of them. "Get your bags and toss them in the back. You're coming with us."

"But—" Jolene protested.

"Do it!"

"California—"

"Yes, sir." Wes tossed the tools into the bed of the truck and ran back for his and Cindy's things.

Nate opened the driver's side door and half urged, half lifted Jolene up onto her seat. He met her gaze, glare for glare, and closed the door behind her.

He pulled off his cap, swatted it against his thigh, then plunked it back onto his head with the bill shading his eyes. Grabbing a blanket from the supplies in back, he dodged out of the way as Wes loaded the suitcases. Once the young man was inside beside his wife, Nate gave him the blanket and climbed in after him, squeezing the four of them in like sardines to shut the door. "Drive."

Jolene gripped the steering wheel in both hands and leaned forward to make eye contact across the couple sandwiched between them. "I do not have to follow your orders."

Nate veed his fingers and held them up. "Two words. Lily Browning."

The reminder was enough to get her to slam the truck into gear, though her chin still tilted at that defiant angle.

"What about driving to San Antonio?" Cindy whined.

"In a couple of hours this road isn't going to be here," Nate advised. "Being late for your honeymoon might be the least of your worries."

There. She was finally scared enough to be quiet. And though Nate felt as guilty as hell for his bullying tactics, if that was the only way he could keep these people safe, then that was what he was going to do.

As Cindy sank back into her seat and snuggled beneath the blanket, Nate reached across Wes to get the radio and report in. It took a couple twists of the dial to find a clear line, and there were still glitches of static by the time he got through to Mitch Kannon.

"Yeah, Mitch. Nate Kellison here." He felt Jolene's wide-eyed gaze beseeching him to keep her accident a secret. He pointed down the road, silently telling her to drive, avoiding those blue eyes. Defiance he could handle. *That* look sucker-punched him in the gut and turned his thinking erratic. "We just stopped to pick up a couple of…" He almost said *kids,* but Wes's earnest expression changed his mind. "A young couple. Their car ran off in the ditch."

"Any injuries?" Mitch asked, his tone conveying a mix of authority and concern.

"Negative."

"Thank God."

"But the car needs more help than we can give them. So we're transporting them to the Rock-a-Bye Ranch with us."

"Understood." Static cut out part of Mitch's answer. "…quite a few evacuees. We're getting more reports of…stranded." Nate was ready to ask him to repeat his message, but the tenor of Mitch's voice changed. "How's Jolene?"

"A little damp."

Mitch laughed. The tension inside the truck ratcheted down a notch as Nate sensed Jolene relax. He breathed easier, too, feeling a bit more like a prince than a bully again. "Do you have an update on the weather?" Nate asked.

He already guessed Mitch's answer.

"I hate it when I'm right. The hurricane turned…report says it's going to make landfall farther south…heading straight for Turning Point."

Nate could fill in the static blanks himself. So could the other three passengers in the truck, judging by their grim expressions.

"The hurricane's going to hit *us?*" Cindy asked,

her meek voice more frightened teenager than disgruntled bride now. She reached for Wes's hand. He took it, put his arm around his wife, squeezed her tight. Good kid.

Good *man*, Nate amended. He looked across the cab at Jolene to offer her what silent comfort he could—if she'd take it.

She nodded, then patted Cindy's knee and explained in a calm, succinct voice, "Turning Point's forty miles inland, so it won't be hit by the full force of the storm. We'll feel the brunt of the winds and the rain. Damon might spawn some thunderstorms or even tornadoes. But we'll get you someplace safe. You'll be fine."

"Wes?" She snuggled closer to her husband.

"I'm right with you, honey. If Mrs. Angel says we'll be safe, we'll be safe." He betrayed his confidence by turning to look at Nate. "Right, sir?"

"Right." Nate pressed the talk button again. "Mitch, we're en route to the Rock-a-Bye again. We're at…" He looked to Jolene for a location.

"About five miles out."

"We're about five miles from our destination," he reported. "Any update on Mrs. Browning's condition?"

"Yeah." More static. Or was that papers rustling? "Ruth! Where's the…Browning?" There was another pause, then, "Her contractions are about ten minutes apart. You'd better book it…her and the kids."

"Did he say ten minutes?" Jolene asked.

Nate felt the truck picking up speed. "Get us there in one piece, Andretti," he warned.

She didn't slow.

"We're on it." Nate had one more question he needed

an answer to, just so he'd know how much worse things were going to get. "When is Damon supposed to make landfall, Mitch?"

Mitch Kannon's grave warning filled the cab of the truck. "We're predicting it'll hit us around midnight."

More static warned them that the storm was building in intensity. Electricity in the atmosphere was already playing havoc with the radio waves.

"Unless that baby's already here, y'all might have to hole up and ride out the storm at the ranch."

"Roger that, Mitch. We'll check in when we can. Kellison out."

He hung up the radio. The only sounds were the grinding of the truck's twisted axle, the spray of gravel and mud beneath the tires, and the endless staccato barrage of rain coming at them from every angle.

Hole up and ride out the storm.

Crazy Texans.

They'd be riding out a damn hurricane.

CHAPTER FOUR

THUNDER RUMBLED in the distance, mimicking the fusillade of silt and gravel hitting beneath the floorboards of the truck. The rain was steady now. Relentless. Inescapable. The ditches were overflowing and it was only a matter of time before the wind or something worse swept across the flat Texas plains.

But right now the world outside seemed more inviting than the world inside the cab of Jolene's truck.

The humid air swallowed up her pensive sigh.

He was rubbing his knee again.

Jolene watched the subtle, yet methodic clench and release of Nate's hand as he dug into the muscles around the joint. It probably didn't help that they were wedged in so tightly that his knee banged against the door with every bounce and jolt.

Not that Nate Kellison had complained.

Of course, they were less than a mile from the Rock-a-Bye's front gate and he hadn't said a word about anything. Not one, despite the chatter among the newlyweds and herself.

He was watching again, studying the movement of the storm, taking note of the dark sky along the horizon to the north—toward her own ranch. He watched Wes and Cindy, too. He'd even reached over to crank up the heat after noticing how Cindy shivered in her sodden wedding dress.

Was that stoic silence—interspersed with bouts of bossing her around—the way he dealt with his pain? Did losing control of a situation give his *handicap,* as he'd called it, a chance to sneak in and take control of him?

Guilt that her actions might have aggravated his "old injury" flared inside her. In a gesture that had become habit of late, she cradled her left hand against her tummy, soothing the baby when she couldn't soothe herself.

She'd lived with guilt all her life. Despite her father's love, she'd grown up with the irrational notion that she should have been someone different, done something better to make her mother love them enough to want to stay.

She should have married Joaquin the first time he'd asked her, but she'd been holding out for some mythic ideal of happily-ever-after. When it became clear that Prince Charming was never going to show his face in tiny Turning Point, she'd settled for caring and being cared for.

If she'd said yes sooner, she might have learned to feel passion for her dear friend. She might have made love with her husband, instead of being the freakish virgin who'd conceived her child in a hospital lab.

If she'd been artifically inseminated sooner, the baby would have been here by now. If she hadn't delayed, there might have been a chance to save Joaquin. She'd have a companion for life instead of a grave to tend.

As though sensing her troubled thoughts, Joaquin, Jr.,

shifted positions in her womb. Gently, she caressed the spot where life was stirring inside her. Her son would never know his father, never know what a kind, good man he had been.

But he'd know her love. Her baby would never lack for that.

If it was enough. If *she* could be enough.

Way too many *if*s.

Jolene rubbed her stomach, unsure whether the baby was restless, or if her own self-doubts were responsible for the queasy feeling rising in her gullet. Heck. Maybe she should blame her oddly introspective mood on the rough road and the weather—or the unsettling presence of that wounded know-it-all from California.

From the corner of her eye, she saw Nate's hand go still. Automatically, hers did as well. She was going to add mind-reader to the list of things that irritated her about the visiting paramedic. While he might not be truly psychic, he had a way of noticing her moods and movements that was distinctly unsettling.

Wes and Cindy cuddled between them, whispering sugary apologies to each other over and over, sneaking kisses. But the honeymooners weren't enough of a distraction to keep Jolene from sensing the ripple of awareness radiating across the truck cab. Goose bumps puckered along her arms and legs, and she knew the sudden sensitivity had nothing to do with the damp clothes that stuck to her skin.

Nate was watching her now. As sure as the touch of his hand, she felt him.

An upward glance gave her a glimpse of whiskey-brown eyes, shaded by that omnipresent ball cap. But his gaze was no less piercing, no less questioning.

She slipped her fingers back to the steering wheel and peered into the dull, drab excuse for daylight outside.

What now? she wanted to shout. Where was she falling short this time? How was she pushing his worry buttons? Did he blame her independence for the ache in his knee?

She gripped the wheel tighter and pressed on the accelerator. It was his own fault! He should have just let her fix the damn tire instead of doing all that lifting and bending.

Of course, when he'd picked her up, she'd gotten absolutely no sense that there was anything weak or disabled or hurting about the man. His chest had been hard and warm against her back, his arm strong and secure.

She'd been startled when the car had shifted. Despite the deceptive gentleness of its movement, thousands of pounds of drifting metal could be unpredictable. She could have been struck or pinned beneath it.

But Nate had saved her. He'd picked her up, lifted her out of harm's way, held her tight. He'd saved her. Saved her baby.

For a second time.

Jolene rubbed her tummy again.

"You okay?" Even though she'd been thinking about him, knew he'd been thinking about her, Nate's low-pitched voice surprised her.

She'd felt edgy from the moment he'd caught her watching him at the fire station. The deteriorating weather, the stupid mistakes she'd made, the close calls they'd had didn't help. But she wasn't about to tell him she wasn't feeling like herself today, that she hadn't felt normal since he'd volunteered to be her shadow-slash-savior for the day.

"I…" It was a weak start to an explanation she hadn't come up with yet. Her stomach suddenly growled, protesting the passage of time since breakfast and reminding her that she was eating for two now. The grumbling sound echoed loudly through the cab, earning a giggle from Cindy and turning Jolene's cheeks red.

Wes grinned. "Somebody's hungry."

Baby Joaquin, at least, had given her an easy, honest out to deflect Nate's concern and depersonalize her thoughts about him. "What a surprise, huh?" Jolene joked. "I guess we're ready for an early lunch."

Wes and Cindy took the bait and laughed. But not Nate. He remained serious as ever. "If Mrs. Browning doesn't have something we can fix, there are power bars in the med kits. We'll get you and the baby fed ASAP."

Funny how he could sound comforting and condescending at the same time. "Despite what you probably think, California, I'm prepared for emergencies like this. I keep snacks in my purse."

Nate twisted his neck, looking into the extended cubby space behind the front seat where she'd stashed her bag. "Where are they? Do you need something right now?"

"I'm fine," she insisted. "*We're* fine. I—"

"Here." He held out a package of cheese and stick crackers from her purse, extended them across the seat like a peace offering.

Jolene slowed the truck and looked down at the strong hand that held the snack out to her. It was a simple gesture, purely practical. Still, a yearning—something unexpectedly needy and all too feminine—surfaced inside her, disrupting her protest. What would it be like to have someone looking out for her and her baby? Especially someone with the considerable caretaking skills Nate Kellison possessed?

What would it be like to put her faith and her future into someone else's hands and know she wouldn't be left alone again?

She slid her gaze up along the sturdy arm and ample shoulder. Even the tanned column of his throat and prominent outline of his jaw indicated strength.

But when she looked into his eyes, she saw no warmth, no emotion whatsoever. They were as unsmiling and serious as ever.

"Eat," he ordered.

Poof. So much for that wayward fantasy. It was probably just hunger, or hormones out of whack, that had allowed her to consider liking—perhaps temporarily lusting after—California Kellison for even one crazed moment.

He sat back, peeled open the package and removed a cracker, handing it off to Cindy, who held it out to Jolene. "Go on," he urged. "Junior needs it."

Practicality won out over wounded pride. Jolene took the cracker from Cindy's fingers and stuffed it into her mouth, chewing around her reluctant thanks. "This should tide me over."

She was just another rescue project to him, another call. Maybe, if she put a positive spin on things, she was a temporary partner he felt obligated to protect.

But she was nothing special.

Too skinny, too annoying, too small town—she would never be anyone special. Especially to a cocky California dude who had no clue how to lighten up.

So she went back to taking care of herself. "I'll eat the rest when we get to Lily's. We're almost there."

Cindy pointed over the dashboard into the rain. "Look out!"

Jolene saw the man a second later. He was stumbling along in his cowboy boots, turning into their path to circle around a soupy bog of mud and water.

"Damn crazy…" Nate muttered.

"Idiot!" Jolene slammed on the brakes, pitching them all forward. Fortunately, with seat belts on—Wes and Cindy sharing one—and the road sucking the tires to a stop, no damage was done. "Everyone okay?" Jolene verified.

A chorus of yeah's and fine's and what-the-hell's answered her as she set the gear into Park and honked the horn.

The man in the road slowly turned, shoving his well-creased Stetson back on his thinning gray hair and squinting into the headlights. Jolene shook her head. She didn't have to be a native Texan to assess the situation. Rail-thin cowboy, decked out in faded bandanna and worn leather chaps, walking the road while a storm brewed around him—and no horse in sight. He'd lost his mount and was hiking back to civilization.

She didn't have to be the man's next-door neighbor, either, to recognize the stoop in the old cowboy's back or the string of colloquial curses rattling off his lips. Standing in front of her was one of Turning Point's most cantankerous characters.

"Deacon Tate." Jolene huffed his name out on a sigh that revealed both irritation and affection.

"Why am I not surprised you know this guy?" Nate grumbled. "Don't any of you Texans have enough sense to stay in out of the rain?"

Jolene ignored the rhetorical question. "Lily said she'd lost contact with him early this morning. His radio's probably with his saddle. Wherever that is."

Deacon, a Rock-a-Bye employee for more years than she'd been alive, had obviously been thrown from his horse. And judging by the way he'd cinched his left arm beneath his belt, at least one of his old bones had been damaged in the fall. Jolene unhooked her seat belt.

"Stay put," Jolene and Nate ordered in unison, each sliding out their respective door and hurrying around the hood of the truck.

Nate was shaking his head and blocking her path by the time they met in the middle of the road. "I can handle this."

She tipped her chin up, squinting against the rain that pelted her face and chilled her skin. "So can I."

"Go finish your snack. Feed your baby."

"When we get to the house." She pointed to the ten-foot-high brick pillars only a few yards away, marking the main entrance to the Rock-a-Bye. She quickly scooted around Nate as he turned to look. Hooking her hand through the crook of Deacon's good arm, she led him toward the relative shelter of the truck. "C'mon, old-timer. No sense in all of us getting soaked to the skin."

"Miz Angel." Deacon would have tipped his hat if he could. "Mighty glad to see ya."

Five strong, insistent fingers closed around her upper

arm and pulled her away. "No sense in you getting soaked, period."

Clasping Jolene in one hand and supporting Deacon in the other, Nate guided them both back to the driver's side of the cab.

"Careful, California." She eyed him over her shoulder, not wanting to struggle too hard with Deacon so close beside her. "I'm starting to think there's some sort of sexual discrimination going on here. That you don't think I can do my job because I'm a woman. Or worse, because I'm pregnant."

"What?" Nate stopped and loosened his grip, instantly freeing her. "There's no…" With a sharp huff of breath, he helped Deacon find a seat on the running board of the truck. Then he straightened, squared his shoulders and leaned in close enough that the bill of his cap shielded her face as well as his own from the rain. "I'm following your father's orders," he articulated between tightly clenched teeth. "Trying to keep you safe. I didn't realize what a daunting task that was going to be when I volunteered." He ticked off her transgressions on his fingers. "You talk too much. You act before you think. You take better care of everybody else than you do yourself or that baby. And it's Nate. Why the hell can't you call me Nate?"

Jolene held his gaze, steamed in it. Caught fire inside and withered in the face of it. She'd been wrong to think this man didn't show any emotion. There was plenty of something—anger, frustration, fear—brewing in those dark eyes.

Fear?

Her self-defense mechanism instantly went on the

fritz. Instinctively, she reached out. To soothe, to comfort. Not quite to touch him, but to finger his collar, to idly straighten the damp material into a pleat it could no longer hold.

What did a take-charge California boy with broad shoulders, steely control and a soul-piercing stare have to be afraid of?

"I didn't really mean to accuse you of anything," she told him. "You just…you tend to be a little on the bossy side. Okay, a lot on the bossy side. I'm used to thinking and doing for myself. I might not be a licensed paramedic like you, but I have eight years of experience doing this kind of thing. I've survived pretty well so far. So have the people I've helped."

A deep sigh expanded his chest beneath her palm. "Maybe you just do things differently down here in Texas. I know you get firefighting and first-aid training as an emergency volunteer. But you insist on taking risks you don't need to. I'm used to the people I work with following procedures and listening to common sense."

"Caution and common sense aren't always the same thing. I'm not going to sit on the sidelines and watch when there's a hurricane on the way and I can do something to help." Jolene's hand settled over the rapid, sure beat of his heart and maintained contact as he exhaled. He stood close enough for her to smell the ozone on his skin, along with the tangy clean scent of the man himself. Lordy. Why did he have to smell so darn delicious? The keener sense of smell she'd enjoyed for the past five months was keeping her from making her point. "I won't… You can't…" Her words seemed to stick in her throat. "I intend to do my job."

"So do I."

Stalemate.

She wanted to argue her skills and independence. She wanted to stroke her fingers across the stern set of his mouth and ease his concern. She wanted to snuggle up against that chest and absorb his warmth and strength.

She did none of those things.

Deacon's embarrassed cough startled them both. "Um, should I stop by when it's a better time for y'all?"

Jolene snatched her hand away.

"Sorry." She and Nate glanced down at the grizzled man's amused smile and apologized in unison.

"I'll go grab a med-kit." Remembering she was here as a trained first responder, not a lovelorn teenager, Jolene turned to the back of the truck.

"Stay put." Nate's touch was almost reluctant on her arm this time. "I'll get it."

Jolene nodded, then turned her attention to Deacon. "What hurts?"

"What doesn't? I don't hit the ground as easy as I used to when my horse puts up a fuss."

Jolene pulled a penlight from her pocket, hiked up her pantlegs and squatted in front of him, doing a cursory check of pupil reaction and inspecting him for any head injuries.

Deacon's reactions were just fine, and he seemed more interested in the curve of her belly as her overalls stretched across her midsection than he did in his own condition. "How's Joaquin, Jr.?" he asked.

Coherent thoughts and speech. A good sign. "He's just fine," Jolene answered, dropping her hand to cradle her tummy. "Though he was kickin' up a fuss a minute ago because I haven't fed him lunch yet."

Deacon nodded. "Old grouses like me and little ones like J.J. like to keep a regular schedule. Get cranky if we don't."

Jolene smiled, as she was meant to, but her focus had already moved on to the bruising and awkward angle of his left forearm.

She seemed to be surrounded by cranky males today.

Nate came up behind her and set the med-kit on the ground beside her before he spoke. "That arm's broken."

"Duh, Sherlock."

The sarcastic response leaked out before she realized that he wasn't expressing doubt over her diagnostic abilities. He was simply stating a fact.

Shrugging in lieu of an apology, Jolene gingerly unhooked Deacon's belt and inspected the break more closely. It took her a minute to realize that Nate had positioned himself in such a way as to block most of the rain that the truck couldn't shield her or her patient from. That simple action gave her a chance to dry Deacon's arm and work more efficiently.

"Where's Buck?" She hoped the question about his horse would distract Deacon while she probed the injury.

He bit out a curse but didn't complain. "Back at the barn, I expect, out of this mess. He got spooked by some lightning, dumped me down a ravine and took off. I hiked to the road instead of heading straight home, since I didn't want to run into that bull on foot. Been walking about an hour."

"And you haven't checked in with Lily?"

"Not since this morning. Been riding over hell and

yonder, looking for that dag-blamed, son of a…" His faded hazel gaze darted up to hers. "Sorry. Rocky broke out of his pen sometime last night."

"Any luck finding him?" She opened the kit and pulled out the supplies to clean the lacerations on his arm.

Deacon muttered a graphic opinion about the bull's behavior. "Sorry, ma'am. I found him, all right. If his stud fees hadn't paid the bills during this drought, I'd have shot him for being such a pain in the ass. Whoops. Sorry."

Jolene grinned. His salty language was a fair trade-off for the pain she must be causing him. "I know Rocky's reputation. Do you think there's any chance of him wandering home by himself?"

Deacon shook his head. "The water's starting to fill all the sloughs and arroyos leading into the Agua Dulce. That bull's got himself stranded in between 'em—if he ain't drowned himself yet. Wouldn't see I wanted to help him. I was trying to get him up to dry land, herd him back to the corral. But all he saw was a cowboy fixed on telling him what to do, and he sure wasn't gonna have none of that. Those danged Santa Gertrudis got too much stubbornness in 'em. Between Rocky and the storm, old Buck couldn't wait to get back to the barn."

Nate shifted on his feet behind her. "Santa Gertrudis. That's a Brahma-Shorthorn cross, right?"

Huh? California knew about Texas cattle?

"Yessir." Deacon tipped his hat back, a glint of admiration in his wrinkled face. "Rocky's the number one S.G. in Texas. You new around these parts?"

"Just visiting. Helping out a friend. I'm Nate Kellison."

"Deacon Tate." Deacon shook his hand without hesitation. Nate had even used the proper pronunciation for Brahma—rhymed with *tamer*. Right away the old cowboy had recognized and respected Nate's expertise.

Jolene was a little slower to come around.

"You know about cattle?" she asked, grabbing the scissors to trim away the remnants of Deacon's sleeve.

"I know about a lot of things."

Like surfing and Tinseltown and overcrowded highways. Right?

"You've been on a ranch before?"

"Yeah."

Water splashed her cheek as he knelt down beside her. His tiny grunt gave the only indication of the strain the position must be putting on his knee. He took the scissors from her hand and tossed the soiled, bloody cloth into the bed of the truck, hurrying along her work. There was more to that *yeah* than Jolene could fathom right now. More to Nate Kellison than she'd given him credit for—more than she'd wanted to give him credit for.

"Isn't it about time for you to get into the truck?" he asked.

"Huh?" She stopped staring at his stern profile and pulled a sling from the kit.

Nate took the sling from her and urged her to move. "You've done a fine job so far. But the rain's picking up."

Fortunately she was still graceful enough to stand up on her own. "It'll go faster if we work together, won't it?"

With a reluctant nod, Nate turned his attention to the broken arm. Though she lacked the shoulders to form as effective a barrier as he had, Jolene situated herself behind him and blocked the rain as much as possible.

"This is just a temporary splint on your arm," Nate

told Deacon. "We'll hold off until we can get some X rays before wrapping you up in something more permanent."

The sure efficiency of Nate's strong hands was an amazing thing to watch, Jolene conceded. He had Deacon cinched up and her imagination thinking about back-rubs and foot massages in no time.

"Anything else hurt, sir?" Nate asked.

Deacon set his hat in place and shook his head, rising to his feet. "It's Deacon, son. I gotta get back and check on Buck, make sure he's in one piece. Oughta check on Miz Browning and the boys, too."

"That's where we're headed. Give you a lift?"

"Looks like you're full-up already."

Cindy knocked on the window before rolling it down. "I can sit on Wes's lap," she offered.

"Who's the Ken and Barbie?" Deacon asked.

"We're collecting strays," Jolene explained, backing out of Nate's way as he repacked the med-kit. "C'mon. We'll find room. We need to get a move on, though. Lily's in labor."

"Well, hell's bells, girl, why didn't you say so? I suppose, since you're comin' to us, there's no way to get her to the hospital."

"Hurricane Damon turned south and is heading right for us. I'm afraid the town already has more evacuees than it can handle, especially without Doc Holland around." She nodded toward Nate. "So Dad sent the cavalry to help out."

"Then what are we sittin' around yappin' about it for?" Fired up with a new purpose, Deacon followed Nate to the bed of the truck and climbed in while the tailgate was down. "That doggone bull can find his own way home through the storm, if he's a mind to. Let's go."

Jolene slipped in behind the wheel and restarted the engine.

Across the barrier of blankets and newlyweds separating them, Nate got in and didn't say a word about the number of *stray puppies* she was collecting today.

And the rain poured down.

A CRY OF BONE-DEEP PAIN echoed throughout the two-story house, momentarily drowning out the rhythmic drumbeat of the rain slapping against the windows now that the wind had picked up. Lily Browning's sob ripped right to the heart of Nate's soul.

Nate splashed cold water on his face and tried to feel anything but halfway useless and way too late.

The twenty-minute trip from Turning Point had taken over two hours. Now, two more hours since their arrival, Lily Browning had dilated to ten centimeters and was burning with the need to push. Cindy Mathis had turned out to be a primo baby-sitter for Lily's three sons, while her new husband, Wes, had willingly gone outside to supply the muscle Deacon needed to secure the barn and nail plywood scraps over the first floor windows of the two-story ranch house.

Jolene had been a rock of support for her friend, holding Lily's hand and breathing with her to help her endure the pain, explaining in succinct detail every step Nate had taken to monitor the baby's progress and prep Lily for delivery.

But something was wrong.

Something was very wrong, and there was no doctor or ambulance to call. There was only Nate. But instead of taking charge and sticking to the rescue routine that had been instilled in him from day one of his paramedic training, Nate felt paralyzed, the image of a dead baby on the side of a California highway frozen in his mind. His ears heard nothing but the sound of an injured mother's distressed cries as she screamed her child's name. His body had numbed to everything but the gut-sick feeling of knowing he hadn't been quick enough, skilled enough, gifted enough to save that baby's life.

Knowing he was no good to Lily or her baby until he could get his head screwed on right, Nate had excused himself and gone into the bathroom for a few minutes, leaving Lily in Jolene's surprisingly capable hands. He'd headed downstairs instead of using the bath off Lily's bedroom because he needed the time. Time and distance and space to catch a deep breath and suppress all those debilitating images again.

He rubbed his hand across his cheeks and jaw now, studying his reflection in the mirror over the sink. He barely recognized the man staring back at him.

The eyes were the same, maybe a little bleary after flying the red-eye and surviving his busy morning. The features were the same, if a tad on the scruffy side, since his last shave had been yesterday morning.

But the light was gone. The spark of confidence he'd once worn like his silver championship belt buckle had dulled beneath the weight of responsibility and guilt and regret.

He couldn't get it right anymore. He couldn't save lives. He'd always be a step behind, a minute too late.

He hadn't stopped Jolene from nearly wrecking her

truck. He'd barely managed to get her to eat anything other than the cheese and crackers from her purse. And he knew the only way he'd get her to take a break and get some rest herself would be to physically carry her out of Lily's room and stand watch over her.

But judging by the itchy need that tickled his palms just thinking about the possibility, Nate had a pretty good idea that touching Jolene Kannon-Angel again would be a bad idea if he wanted to maintain a professional distance. Something about her stubborn ways fired him up. Something about those blue eyes and soft skin stirred an ache in his body. Something about her ultrafeminine shape and dazzling smile wakened him to possibilities he'd never imagined before.

But a man who was a step behind and a minute late, snared in the mistakes of his past, had no business imagining anything beyond getting his job done right.

Shutting off the water, Nate blinked and looked a little harder at his reflection. "You can do this," he lectured himself. He'd delivered babies before, survived plenty of disasters—natural and man-made. "You have to do this."

With a deep breath, he pushed aside fears and aches and wants and needs, and planted himself firmly in the moment at hand. Nate opened the door and headed for the stairs, leaving his emotions behind.

Lightning flashed, momentarily flooding the entryway with brilliant white light, before disappearing again into the haze of the storm-shrouded afternoon. Thunder boomed a second later, rattling the windows and masking Lily's sob from the floor above.

"Jolene, this isn't right. She's coming. I can feel... ohhhh!"

"Shh." Jolene used soft, soothing words, gentling Lily in the same tone she'd used with her own baby after nearly wrecking the truck. That same tone gentled Nate's raw nerves and helped the tortured images in his brain recede a little.

He hit the first step, ready to work.

"Oh, my God." He lifted his head, instantly attuned to the hushed desperation in Jolene's voice. "That's a foot."

A foot? Lily's baby should be crowning by now.

Breech.

No wonder Lily was in such pain. No wonder the delivery was taking so long. If they'd had the right equipment, the proper facilities, he would have seen the problem before now.

Hell. He was more than a few steps behind on this one.

"Nate!" Jolene was shouting now. "I need you! Nate!"

Nate was already moving, damning his weak knee as he took the stairs two at a time. It wasn't just the panic in her voice that urged him to run. It wasn't the fear of losing another child under his care that drove him to Jolene's side.

She'd called him Nate.

CHAPTER FIVE

"SHE'S READY TO DELIVER, but the baby's turned around."

Jolene met Nate at the door, searched his face for the control and confidence he had in such ample supply. She allowed herself one moment of relief, knowing he was there.

The tiny foot she'd glimpsed in the birth canal had frightened her. She'd been scared for Lily, for the baby's safety. And for one irrational instant, she'd been scared for her own unborn child. She'd never before delivered a baby in breech position. Screw her independence, her need to succeed on her own terms. How could she guarantee their safety? How could she guarantee the health and safety of little Joaquin if she couldn't even manage this?

Irrational.

Overwhelmed.

She'd cried out for help and Nate Kellison had answered the call. He paused in the doorway, grasped her shoulder and gave her a gentle squeeze.

Sweet relief.

Reporting Lily's stats, she fell into step behind him as he dashed in. His limp was more pronounced. His knee seemed to be bothering him more and more as the day dragged on, but the urgent purpose in his stride refused to concede to any pain. "Lily?"

"Oh, God." Lily's plea was a ragged, desperate cry. "I need to push!"

"Can you hold off for just a minute longer?" Nate asked, pulling a clean pair of latex gloves from the medkit and adjusting Lily's position on the bed.

"I'll try."

"The baby dropped, but he didn't turn." Jolene took hold of Lily's hand and let her friend squeeze as tightly as she needed to. "Easy, Lily. I'm right here with you. Nate's going to help us. Right?"

Flecks of doubt darkened Nate's eyes, but they disappeared before Jolene could question him.

"You bet." Nate sounded confident, focused.

Jolene nodded, absorbing his determination. His brand of *serious* looked mighty reassuring for a change. The practiced efficiency with which he donned a stethoscope to listen to the baby's heartbeat, and palpated Lily's rigid abdomen didn't hurt, either. His brown eyes flicked up to hers and Jolene latched on to the strength she saw there.

"See if you can distract her a bit and help her relax," Nate instructed her. "I'll have to time this around her contractions."

Obeying without protest, Jolene took a deep breath and tapped into her own strength. Nate sat on the stool they'd moved to the end of the bed earlier and went to work. Jolene dipped a washcloth into the bowl of cool water on the bedside table and wrung out the excess. Then she pressed the cloth to Lily's lips and urged her to suck the moisture. She talked about the first thing that popped to mind, then kept talking, holding her friend's hand, massaging gentle circles against her back and shoulders to distract her while Nate reached in to help the baby.

"Rocky's turned out to be a real pain in the neck, hasn't he," Jolene said.

Lily closed her eyes and nodded. "That bull's both a blessing and a curse. Won more prizes, sired dozens of the hardiest stock in all of Texas…" Her breath caught.

"Easy, Lily," Nate urged, rubbing one hand against her belly. "Don't push yet."

"But I'm burning—"

"We're going to get this guy lined up and then he'll be out in no time."

"Guy?" Lily's eyes, damp with sweat and tears, popped open. "Is it another boy? I wanted—"

"Shh," Jolene cooed, squeezing Lily's hand and insisting her friend focus on her instead of the pain or any regrets about adding a fourth son to her rambunctious posse. "What makes Rocky such a curse?" Jolene grinned, demanding Lily's attention. "Besides giving your ranch hands a workout."

Lily grasped at the topic. "Rocky's worth thousands of dollars to us. Did Deacon get him back? Oh Lord, if I lose him to this storm, Gabe's gonna kill me."

"Gabe's only going to be worried about you and the baby." Of that, Jolene was certain. Gabe and Lily Browning had been an old married couple the moment they got engaged. Devoted to each other in the way Jolene had wished her own parents had been in love, the way she wished she and Joaquin had been able to be.

"If Rocky's as smart and ornery as Deacon says he is, that bull will be just fine."

"But a hurricane?" Lily's breathing had quickened and gone shallow. She was desperate to push again. "Even that—" she winced "—damn bull…can't survive on his own in those kinds of wind. He needs…shelter. We'll lose—"

"We'll find him," Jolene promised, tuning in to Lily's desperation and wanting to ease it in whatever way she could. "We'll take care of Rocky. You just worry about your little—"

"Got it. Push now, Mrs. Browning." Nate's stiff order interrupted them. "Push if you can."

"God, yes."

Lily scrambled up onto her elbows. Jolene propped the pillows behind her and supported her back. "You can do it, Lily. Take a deep breath." She held hers along with her friend. "Push."

In just a few minutes, the thunder outside was drowned out by the wail of a newborn baby. Plenty healthy from the sound of things.

"Oh, God. Thank you, God," Lily breathed. "How is he? Is he okay?"

Tears pricked Jolene's eyes and she whispered a prayer of thanks herself. She tried to peek around Lily's raised knees, but knew her first priority was to help their patient lie down as comfortably as possible.

Nate tied off the cord, suctioned the tiny airways and wrapped the infant in the clean towels Jolene had gathered. When he rose, the bundle looked tiny, yet infinitely secure, cradled in his sturdy arms. Jolene blinked, sending a tear down her cheek.

She knew the feeling.

"Here you go, Mrs. B." Nate circled the bed and laid the bundle of baby on Lily's chest. "You wouldn't be looking for a little girl, would you?"

"What? A girl?" Lily panted a moment in shock. Then a sudden energy suffused her, lighting up her expression. She quickly unwrapped the baby, verified the truth for herself, then swaddled her tiny daughter tight. She kissed the baby's head over and over. "My little girl. At last. Amber Renee Browning. My sweet little girl."

Lily snatched Nate's wrist and tugged him down to kiss his cheek. "Thank you, thank you."

Was that a blush turning the tips of his ears pink? Jolene wondered.

Nate pulled away. "You did all the work, ma'am. You did a fine job."

Lily beamed, though whether it was in response to the compliment or the sheer joy of finally getting the daughter she'd wanted for so long, Jolene couldn't tell.

"Is she healthy?" Lily asked.

Nate nodded. "As far as I can tell. All the fingers and toes are there. She's pink and plump and has plenty to say."

"Oh, yes," Lily cooed to her newborn. "Mommy loves you, too. Daddy's going to spoil you rotten. And you have three big brothers you'll have to keep in line."

As mother and daughter got acquainted, Nate and Jolene faded out of the picture for a moment. Breathing easier herself, Jolene hugged her tummy and the baby inside. They were okay. Everyone was okay. And they had California here to thank for it.

Without thinking, she reached for Nate's hand, and laced her fingers through his. "Thank you."

If the touch had startled him, he never let on. He turned to study her, tightening his grip around hers as if it was the most natural thing in the world for two strangers who barely knew each other and who'd butted heads more often than not to come together to share this miraculous moment.

He really did have beautiful eyes. Eyes that saw more than they should, perhaps. Jolene was so caught up in the warmth there that she didn't see him lift his hand to her face. But she felt his gentle touch against her skin and savored the tender stroke of his finger along her cheek. He wiped away the trail of her tear and another fell to replace it.

Nate frowned. "You okay?"

"Hormones run amok," she laughed, knowing something much more profound had just happened here. The protective distance separating them had vanished, and she still wanted to be closer to him. She soaked in his caring. She longed to offer her own. That's when she noticed the moisture glistening in his dark lashes. "You?"

Nate swallowed hard and Jolene's gaze darted to his Adam's apple bobbing along the column of his throat. She waited expectantly, hurting at the anguish he obviously felt.

She reached up, her fingertips drifting across the tight set of his mouth. His lips parted beneath her touch, and his warm breath brushed past her fingers in a subtle, heated caress that stirred something more than compassion inside her. But he released her, denying her an answer, rejecting her comfort, acknowledging his emotions by covering them up. Keeping them in check. Again.

"I need to finish up," he announced, returning to the

end of the bed and pulling on a new pair of gloves so he could secure the afterbirth and do some suturing. "See to the baby's stats, will you? And one of us needs to call in a sit rep."

"I'll handle the situation report, California." There. That got a rise out of him, judging by the quick jerk of his head as he glanced her way. But he studiously returned to his work, forgoing his insistence she call him Nate. Jolene felt no satisfaction, only more frustration. How many times did she have to tell herself she shouldn't be feeling *anything* for a man who was destined to leave her? "I want to check on Dad, anyway."

Biting her tongue to keep from asking what it was about babies that tore him up so, why he felt it necessary to be a robot when it came to revealing emotions, Jolene reluctantly lifted Amber Renee from Lily's arms. She measured and weighed the girl. Put a cap and newborn diaper on her. Made a footprint and filled out the preliminary paperwork. By the time she'd returned the sleeping infant to her mother's arms, Nate was cleaning up.

At Lily's request, Jolene headed downstairs and informed Gabe, Jr., Aaron and Seth that they could go meet their new baby sister. They charged up the stairs with Cindy in tow. The storm outside grew noisier as the inside of the house quieted. Jolene found Deacon taking a well-deserved snooze in the recliner and covered him with an afghan.

Wes stamped in ahead of a gust of wind and rain and slammed the door in the mudroom off the back of the kitchen. "Man, it's a bitch out there," he complained, peeling off the poncho he'd borrowed from Deacon.

When he saw Jolene standing there with a towel to dry off with, he turned three shades of pink. "Sorry, ma'am."

"Don't apologize. Come on in. Your wife made us all a late lunch."

"Cindy cooked?"

Jolene bit back a smile at the stunned, hopeful look on his face. They were such newlyweds, and—she felt the tinge of an ache taking hold at the small of her back—so, so young. "Peanut butter sandwiches, I'm afraid. But there's plenty of them."

She tossed him the towel and returned to the kitchen to pour them each a glass of milk. "Did you get everything secured?"

"Yes, ma'am." Wes took off the boots he'd borrowed and tiptoed into the kitchen. "I'm sure glad we're here instead of stranded out on the side of that road. I hope my brother's car hasn't floated out to the Gulf yet."

"Me, too. Here. Sit." She placed two sandwiches, a stack of pretzels and an apple in front of him, then sat down to eat her own meal.

She'd set a place for Nate, but he was either still cleaning upstairs or simply avoiding her. Something had shifted between them as they'd worked together to deliver Lily's baby. It had taken his skills and strength, her caring and alertness to bring Amber Browning into the world. But he'd dropped his guard for a few timeless moments; she'd glimpsed a man wounded in ways a simple limp could never explain.

And she'd wanted him. Needed him. Cried out for him because she'd been scared and Nate Kellison seemed like the most solid, reliable anchor she could cling to in the midst of all the chaos around her. And when he'd held her hand and rejoiced in the moment of Amber's birth, when he'd touched her cheek and cared about her tears, she'd wanted to turn to him for something more.

She'd wanted him to hold her. To kiss her. To truly smile.

But he'd closed up, given her an order and walked away instead.

Jolene gulped down half her milk, concentrating on the cold liquid sliding down her throat, cooling her frustrations and curiosity. Damn the man, anyway, for making her care. He was welcome to take his attitude and his hurts and those soulful brown eyes back to California and get the heck out of her life before she got to thinking how nice it might be if he really would stay.

Her life would be a lot easier if she went back to relying on herself and worrying about the one man who had never let her down.

Crossing to the phone beside the mudroom entrance, Jolene lifted the receiver. Nothing. No dial tone, no busy signal. Nothing.

She hung up and glanced over at Wes Mathis, who was making quick work of the lunch she'd served him. "Are the phone lines down?"

"Mmm…" Wes swallowed the last of his apple. "Yeah. Deacon said service went out about an hour ago. As hard as the wind's blowing, I'll bet there are lines down all over the place." He got up and carried his plate to the sink. "I'm surprised we haven't lost electricity yet. Deacon had me pull the generator out of the shed, just in case."

"I didn't know it had gotten so bad." She took out her

cell phone and punched in her father's number. At least the cell towers were still transmitting signals. "It's ringing. Thank God."

For the first time that day, Jolene wondered about her own ranch—whether she should be there boarding up windows and setting up generators as well. Had she remembered to lock the doors and secure the paddock gate? With luck the horses would have enough sense to go inside the barn. She should be there to make sure flooding didn't contaminate the well, to ensure Joaquin Angel's legacy to their son wasn't washing down river or blowing away in the wind.

But she'd been needed here. Her father had needed her help. Wes and Cindy had needed someone. So had Deacon.

The phone kept ringing.

"Hey, I'm gonna go up and meet the new baby," Wes said. "If that's okay?"

"Sure." She waved Wes on his way when he hesitated. "I'll clean up here." A faint tension settled across her shoulders after he zoomed upstairs. "C'mon, Dad. Pick up."

The quiet of the kitchen proved little barrier against the growing fury of the storm outside and Jolene's nerves were stretched beyond taut. The wind whipped branches against the siding and hummed through the eaves overhead. Rain pelted the roof and the temperature was steadily dropping. The carpet of goose bumps that prickled her arms had become as constant a companion as the baby she carried inside her.

Right on cue, little Joaquin tumbled over inside her, as if sensing his mother's concern. Jolene cupped her belly and rubbed gentling circles through the now stiff denim overalls. "Hang in there, sweetie," she soothed. "Mama's going to keep you safe. I'm just worried about Grandpa."

And the Double J. And the storm. And Amber Browning's future. And that damn Californian who'd disrupted her life in the first place.

She'd nearly disconnected after the eighth ring.

"Jolene?"

Of course, he'd read her number on his phone. Her breath rushed out in a sigh of hope and relief. "Dad?"

"Are you okay?" they asked in unison.

She listened to Mitch Kannon's deep, calming breath. Felt it calm her as well. "I'm fine, hon."

"Me, too."

"Please tell me you're somewhere safe."

She could hear noises in the background now, and wondered if her father was working an accident scene or if the evac center was being overrun. "We're still at the Rock-a-Bye ranch. Deacon and the newlyweds are set for now, though Deacon will need an X ray. The Brownings are fine, but Rocky's still on the loose."

"That's gonna cost them if they lose him. I hope no one winds up with a runaway bull in their backyard. I don't suppose the weather's helping his temperament any."

She hadn't thought of the danger the bull could pose to anyone else. One more thing to worry about on a growing list. "I'm glad I could reach you on my cell. The static's so bad we can't get the radio to work, and now the phone lines are down."

"That's pretty much the status here. We're getting reports of power outages around the county. Flooding.

Bridges out. Wind damage. Cars off the road. Hell, I've even got a missing Scout troop—over there." Mitch addressed someone at the other end of the line. Jolene could overhear him directing the placement of cots at the fire station. By the time he was back on the line, she knew he had his hands full and didn't need to be shouldering any of her burden as well. "I'm damn glad the California volunteers showed up," Mitch said. "There's no way we could handle all the calls we're getting by ourselves."

Jolene looked up at the ceiling, envisioning Nate's skilled hands. "I hate to admit it, but I'm glad Kellison was with me. The baby was breech and I couldn't get her turned around."

"Her?" She could hear the smile in her father's voice. "Did Lily finally get her little girl?"

Jolene discovered she could smile now, too, and was glad she could offer her father some happy news. "Amber Renee. Twenty inches long, seven pounds, three ounces, and as mouthy as her mother. You should see how crazy the boys are about her already."

"Yeah, baby girls have a way of getting to the men in their lives."

The personal message in his wistful tone comforted her and reminded her of the special bond they shared. "Have you had a chance to sit down and catch your breath, Dad? Did you eat lunch?"

"I'll catch my breath once this hurricane blows over and I know my people are safe. And yes, Ruth made sure I ate a sandwich and had some coffee."

"Good for her." If the dispatcher was a tough enough cookie to raise three teenage sons on her own, then she could keep Mitch Kannon in line. Jolene breathed a little easier, knowing someone closer to home was looking after her father. "Well, I won't keep you. I just wanted to report in. Is there anything you need me to do?"

"You couldn't if you wanted to. Sheriff Boone said the main highway's flooded out near the river, and you told me the backroads were already impassable." She recognized the deep breath that preceded a fatherly warning. "So you stay put at the Rock-a-Bye. Don't try to come into town until this thing blows itself out. You think this storm front is bad, just wait until the real thing hits us tonight."

Stay put?

Her feet were already dancing with the antsy need to help, to take action. She needed to do *something*. "We won't head for town," she promised, knowing she could never lie to her father outright.

But she could check her own ranch. She could try to recover Rocky for Gabe and Lily.

"Jolene?" Mitch Kannon was no fool. "Remember, you're responsible for two people now."

She hugged her belly. "I know. I promise, nothing will happen to your grandson."

"Jolene? Put Kellison on the line." He knew her thoughts were already jumping ahead to her next rescue mission. "Don't you go off on some—"

"Mitch?" Ruth's voice interrupted the call. Papers rattled, furniture crashed and someone cussed in the background. Apparently Turning Point had another emergency that required her father's attention.

Jolene knew the town was in good hands. "I love you, Dad."

"Love you, too." He didn't want to ring off, but he had to. "Call when you can."

"I will."

As a flurry of activity filled the fire station, Jolene hung up and stuffed the phone into her pocket. Reassured as she was by her father's voice, she knew her work wasn't finished. There was still work to be done before Hurricane Damon struck. And more once he had passed. She might not be able to get to town to help her father, but she could make a difference here.

Lily was worried about Rocky. Deacon couldn't work with his arm. Wes was no cowboy, and the boys needed Cindy.

The Rock-a-Bye needed its bull to survive.

And there was nothing Jolene could do here but wait.

Sit on her hands and wait for Hurricane Damon to hit and pass.

She swallowed hard, missing her father, missing Joaquin, missing the life that would never be hers, a life like Lily's.

She couldn't just sit and wait and worry.

She felt cocooned inside the rambling house, trapped by feelings she didn't want to have.

Stuffing the last of the sandwich into her mouth, Jolene grabbed the poncho Wes had worn and slipped out the back door.

"CRAZY TEXAS WOMAN."

Nate grumbled a curse between his teeth and shifted the white bassinet onto his hip as he glared out the bedroom window. With Wes's help, he was moving Lily and Amber and all the necessary supplies down to the more secure main floor to ride out the storm with the menagerie of survivors they'd collected throughout the day.

But apparently Mitch Kannon's darling daughter didn't intend to join them.

Jolene looked more like demon than angel as she dashed from the back of the house, past the empty horse paddock and into the barn. *Fast* seemed to be the only speed she functioned in. Maybe she'd run track in school. Maybe she hated to get wet. Or maybe she was just used to having to stay a step or two ahead of trouble. Even five months pregnant, she covered the distance like a gazelle.

An urgency clenched his muscles, sharpened his senses. The rapid pulse, the hyper-awareness—the challenge staring him in the face—all reminded him of the adrenaline rush he used to get each time he climbed down into the gate on the back of a bull and braced himself to ride out into the rodeo ring.

Nate shook his head at the notion. He'd thought those days were over. He was a sober, mature adult now. Caretaker to his family. Guardian of their heritage. Protector and healer for the citizens of Courage Bay, California.

But then, he'd never met a woman like Jolene before.

And while the younger, freer part of him enjoyed that rush of feeling again, the sager, more practical man he'd become knew that his blood pressure probably couldn't take much more of the *challenge* Jolene presented.

The barn door slammed shut behind her and Nate let the curtains close. He breathed deeply to assuage the grip of fear and frustration and utter destiny that strangled his heart.

Time to go rescue his charge again.

CHAPTER SIX

NATE BLINKED THE RAIN from his lashes and swiped the water from his face, ignoring the wind catching the barn door and slapping it shut behind him. His palm rested on the scratch of his beard as his eyes adjusted to the dim light of the barn's interior. The scents of hay, leather and horses soothed him and sparked familiar memories.

But no way was he relaxing.

The stamp of hooves and creak of leather tack directed his steps.

He sighed heavily as he caught a glimpse of a limp blond ponytail and bright red poncho moving beside a sorrel horse.

This just got better and better.

"You *do* know there's a hurricane on its way, right?"

"Dad said it shouldn't hit us until later tonight."

So, of course, she had saddled a horse.

Damn crazy...

Stalking toward the row of stalls with as much purpose as his throbbing knee allowed, Nate saw a sweet little curve of denim-clad rump, and a long line of leg as Jolene slipped her foot into the stirrup and swung up onto the horse.

"I don't think so."

He tugged on her arm, palmed a handful of her hip and pulled her down.

"Hey! What—?"

"Not this time, lady." With the baby to protect and the unreliability of his leg, he pulled her bottom straight into his chest and let her slide down the length of him.

"Put me—!"

The friction of wet denim and firm bodies was pure, sweet torture. Nate's groin leaped to embarrassing life, demanding some sort of satisfaction for the paces she was putting him through.

But as soon as Jolene's boots touched the ground, she twisted in his grasp.

"Oh, no, you don't." Nate backed her against the horse so she couldn't squirm away. "I promised your father I'd keep you safe."

Her cheeks flushed with a tantalizing heat. "I—"

"You're pregnant. You need your rest."

"I feel fine."

She felt warm and soft and female and tempting wedged against his chest and thighs. "I intend to keep that promise with or without your help. You are not getting on that horse."

Her eyes blazed blue as a clear, coastal dawn. But the moment she started to argue, his gaze dropped to her pink, pretty mouth. It was talking. Again. "I know what I'm doing. I grew up in Texas. I've ridden horses forever. You have no right to boss—"

Nate palmed the back of her neck, tipped her face up to his and kissed her, silencing the words intended to push them apart.

Startled, Jolene gasped, seeming to draw the breath

right from his chest. That soft little sound primed him, sparked something wild and reckless deep inside him. He felt her hands at his shoulders, bracing herself, digging in, holding on when she should be pulling away.

The years fell away from his tortured old soul and his ears pounded with the flare of pent-up needs and desires.

Jolene was on her toes and Nate was holding her close.

Cold, wet clothes and hot, instant passion beaded the tips of her breasts against his aching chest. The fertile swell of her belly and the life growing inside thrust against his stomach, humbling him. Her luscious body roused, yet at the same time soothed every basic male instinct he possessed.

There was little finesse on either of their parts—noses bumped, feet tangled, water dripped from poncho and cap. But her open mouth was warm, her tongue a delicious rasp, her lips giving and demanding beneath his. The tension that had yin and yanged between them all day long seemed to gather itself and focus its heat into this one time-stopping kiss.

The storm outside melted away. There was no hurricane, no emergency, no lives waiting to be saved.

There was only the two of them.

In all his life, Nate had never shared a kiss like this. He felt sure he could live a dozen lifetimes and never know a kiss like this one. With this woman.

Joaquin Angel's woman.

Whoa.

Nate jerked at the unsettling thought. Jolene tensed, pushed against his chest. Her horse shifted, knocking her into Nate. Knocking a chink in the raw need that consumed him, giving his much-touted common sense a chance to flood into his brain.

With a wrenching sigh, Nate lifted his mouth and released her, ending the kiss as abruptly as it had begun. He held his hands out to either side, signalling the end to that crazy, wild ride.

"That...shouldn't have happened," were the best words of apology he could summon at the moment.

He was still pinned by the drowsy passion in those deep blue eyes, still caught by the spell of those sassy lips, made rosy and swollen by the brand of his mouth. He was still drowning in the scents of home and heat that clung to her hair and radiated from her damp skin.

"You kissed me." Jolene's chest rose and fell with the same deep, uneven gasps that marked his own breathing.

Guilty as charged. "Yeah. I did. And, uh, you kissed me back."

"Men don't..." Her voice trailed off. She lowered her gaze to a spot near his chin.

Nate noted the sudden pallor in her cheeks. He frowned at the uncharacteristic confusion in her tone. "Men don't what?"

"Not even Joaquin. We never..." She licked her tongue along the rim of her lips as if finding something unfamiliar there. Nate had to look away. There was something completely innocent and totally seductive in the way she tasted herself.

"Never what?" Despite the interest swelling behind his zipper, he reminded himself this was apology time, not round two of kissing his frustrations into submission. "I didn't hurt you, did I? I'm sorry if I overstepped any boundaries. I imagine you're still grieving—"

She snapped her attention back to him, perplexed and alert. "Why did you kiss me?"

Huh? Nate studied the disbelief in her expression. He didn't think this was about intruding on grief or overstepping boundaries. She hadn't recognized his lusty response to her. Wasn't aware that she'd given it back in spades. Had it been that long since he'd kissed a woman?

"California?" Her fingers pinched the hair on his chest as she clutched a fistful of his shirt, urging him to answer.

"Ow." He gently plucked her hand away, hating the nickname but resigning himself to the distance it forced between them. He splayed her fingers apart and slipped his in between, binding them in a more comforting, less painful position against his chest. "It seemed like a good idea at the time. It's been a long couple of days for me. I acted without thinking and just did what felt right."

"So you'd do it again?" Her fingertips curled around his. Was that hope in her eyes? Or trepidation?

Nate honestly didn't know how to answer. He hadn't come to Texas looking for anything beyond the chance to do his job. But he'd found a sexy, confounding angel who pushed buttons in him he never realized he had. Yeah, he'd kiss her. He stroked his thumb across the backs of her fingers. Even the skin there was smooth like velvet. He'd touch her again. Hold her. Do whatever it took to see her beautiful smile and keep her safe.

Safe. Hell. Nate's out-of-control libido came to a grinding halt. He shouldn't be having this conversation. He was here to make sure she got back to her father in one piece, not to piece together a relationship with her. She was so young and full of energy, she probably wouldn't even be interested in a relationship with a gimpy old soul like him, anyway.

Steeling himself, Nate gave Jolene the only answer he could under the circumstances. "No. That won't happen again."

Her audible gasp cut deep into his conscience. She was either insulted or relieved. "I…well…" Jolene snatched her hand away as if the appendage had betrayed her. She rubbed her belly and tilted her chin. Nate braced himself. The fire was back and she picked up the argument right where they'd left off. "Well, good. I have things to do, anyway. You'd better keep it in check next time, Kellison."

He bit down on the impulse to defend himself. She was right. He couldn't lose control like that again. One of them had to be responsible. As usual, he volunteered for the job.

Before she could make good on whatever foolhardy idea she'd hatched, Nate reached around her shoulder, picked up the reins of the sorrel gelding and retied him to the stall gate.

"What were you doing with Sonny, anyway?" he asked, reading the name-plate beside the stall. "Please don't tell me you were going after that bull in this weather."

Oddly enough, the abrupt change in topic didn't seem to phase her a bit. But then, he was quickly learning to expect the unexpected from this woman. "I want to get back to the Double J and make sure I've battened down all the right hatches."

"Is that so?" Removing the heavy bags she'd draped behind the saddle, Nate peeked inside to find a variety of tools and supplies that could mean only one thing. Her heart might be in the right place, but she had no sense of survival. "And if you happen to run into Rocky along the way, you'll just herd him back here before checking the old homestead?"

When he reached for the lariat she'd draped over the saddle horn, Jolene tried to snatch it from his grasp. "Look. I don't know how they do things out in California, but down here in Texas, neighbors help each other. Lily's a good friend. If there's something I can do to help—"

"I know." He'd heard this argument before and still didn't like it. "*You're* going to do it. Isn't it enough that you helped deliver her baby? You made sure her children were taken care of and that Deacon had a chance to play grandpa. You've done more than most already. In California, we appreciate that kind of dedication and compassion, too. But you don't have to personally handle every problem on the planet. Now let go of the rope and go back to the house."

"But Lily still needs—"

"Go back to the house."

"What about my ranch?"

"Jolene."

Nate squared off and held on until she conceded this tug-of-war that was more about stubborn wills than physical strength. Lightning charged the air outside and flashed through the cracks around the barn's doors and windows. An answering smack of thunder rattled the clapboard walls and Sonny danced between the two of them.

On the rumbling drumbeat that followed, Jolene released her grip on the rope. She could damn him with those big blue eyes all she wanted. He'd already surrendered to the inevitable.

Jolene Kannon-Angel had that effect on him—made him do crazy things. Made him want things he shouldn't.

When she turned away to unsaddle Sonny, he went to work. Searching the next few stalls, Nate found Deacon's horse, Buck. He passed another sorrel, then paused to scratch the inquisitive nose of a tall, muscular bay named Checker. He stroked the dark, red-brown hair along the quarter horse's neck and flicked his fingers through the black mane. The big gelding would suit his purpose just fine.

"You'll do," he whispered. "Won't be easy, though." The horse bobbed his head, as if agreeing to the unspoken challenge.

"I really should check the Double J." He heard Jolene moving behind him. "Joaquin left it to me so his son would always have a home. It's my responsibility to take care of it."

Nate found a blanket and saddle for the bay and let her talk while he worked. He'd lasso her and haul her into the house over his shoulder if she wouldn't listen to reason. "There's still that pesky hurricane, remember? Would your husband want you to risk your life or your son's?"

"Then I have to get there before the hurricane does."

"No, you don't." Nate slipped the reins between his fingers and swung up into the saddle. He tested the limited flexibility of his knee, but already felt some relief just taking his weight off the joint. With a click of his tongue and a gentle nudge, he turned the bay toward the doors and tipped the bill of his cap to Jolene. "*I'll* go."

That tempting mouth dropped open and she eyed him as if he'd just sprouted wings. "*You* know how to ride a horse?"

"Looks that way. If I'm not back here before Damon hits, don't come looking for me until it blows over. Understand?"

"But, how…?"

Nate almost grinned at her incredulity. She'd thought he was a fish out of water. *She* was the only thing he didn't know how to handle here. "I grew up on a ranch. Competed in the rodeo until a bull busted up my knee in the ring. By the way, for your information, I know a helluva lot more about riding than I do about surfing." When he reached the door, he leaned down and pushed it open. Horizontal rain instantly pelted him like hundreds of cold slaps in the face. "Hell."

Checker shied beneath him, but Nate tightened his grip and reminded the horse who was boss. The next chapter in this crazy adventure was about to begin. "You're northeast of here a couple of miles, right?"

"More like three." Too late, he realized Jolene had been repacking her gear instead of putting Sonny back in his stall. Once she remounted, she spurred her horse and bolted past him into the storm. "We're a team today, right?"

"Damn it, Jolene!" Nate called out to her. "The whole idea is for you to stay put, stay safe and stay out of trouble." But the wind swept away his words.

Or so he thought.

Jolene had already circled beyond the paddock. She glanced over her shoulder and taunted him as she became little more than a blur of red and gold amidst the camouflaging gusts of wind and rain. "You can't make me if you can't catch me!"

"Oh, I'll catch you," Nate muttered beneath his breath.

He'd made a promise to her father. And to himself.

He paused just long enough to latch the barn behind him before digging his heels into the bay's sides. Adrenaline screamed in his veins, matching the force of the elements beating down around him—matching the lead-with-her-heart will of one crazy, stubborn, remarkably kissable Texas woman.

The chase was on.

"THAT'S ROCKY?" Nate asked, reining his horse in beside Jolene to study the arroyo turned river that cut across their path.

"That's Rocky."

The runaway bull bellowed and threw himself against the bank of the flooded gulley, desperately trying to pull his massive weight out of the chest-deep water that raced past him. But the red, weeping wounds on his rust-colored hide told of the twisted barbed wire that had tangled in his legs and trapped him as the water rose around him.

Nate shook his head. "This is not good."

He and Jolene were both breathing hard after a wild ride across the perimeter of the Rock-a-Bye Ranch into Double J territory. Their chests rose and fell in deep gasps that matched the rhythm of the horses' restless pawing and periodic efforts to shake the water from their skin. Jolene's wind-whipped cheeks provided the brightest spots of color in a landscape where shrouds of rain turned land and sky into one endless gray horizon.

"Not good at all."

Jolene had given up trying to keep the poncho's hood up over her head. The rain had turned her hair a dark gold, and rivulets ran down her face from every loose strand plastered to her forehead. She shoved the tendrils away from her eyes, giving him a glimpse of the fear and compassion there. "We have to help him."

"He may not let us," Nate warned. But he was already assessing the force of the wind, the speed and depth of the instant river. The physical strength he had left after too much Texas and too little sleep.

Jolene raised her hand to shield her eyes from grit blowing on the tornadic gusts of air from the east. The sixty to seventy mile per hour winds probably marked the leading edge of Hurricane Damon. That meant the weather and Rocky's chances of survival—and their own—were only going to get worse.

"I wonder how long he's been trapped there. Maybe he's been weakened by the struggle," Jolene suggested. "If he's tired, it might make him halfway amenable to being helped."

Might. Halfway. Half a bull was still a mighty dangerous adversary to tangle with.

The animal's mournful bellowing didn't seem to phase the horses, but it was obviously having an effect on Jolene's compassionate heart. "If we cut him free, maybe he can get himself out."

"If he'll let me get that close." The last time Nate had gone head-to-head with an angry bull had nearly cost him his life. It *had* cost him his career. And it had damn well handicapped his entire perception of life—how precious it was, how easily it could be thrown away.

A soft hand on his thigh tore him from his thoughts. He glanced down at Jolene's long, capable fingers—strong in intent, yet timid in their touch. He looked up into her eyes. She squinted against the wind and debris, but he saw no fight there. "You said a bull did the damage to your leg. Are you afraid of him?"

When she spoke in that same tender voice she used to soothe her baby, Nate understood how this woman could create a loving home—full of bright smiles and warm hugs, compassion and support, with strong roots that went right down into the Texas soil. All the good things a man wanted to hold on to and protect with his life.

Something he refused to name shifted inside him, and he recognized his longing to be a part of that world, so like the one he'd lost when his parents had died. The one he'd lost a second time when Grandpa Nate had passed away. The one he'd been unable to rediscover since his brother and sister had moved on with lives of their own.

But he was quickly learning that this woman would be just as kind, just as concerned to a stranger as she would be to the man she loved. Nate buried his own yearnings and accepted her compassion for what it was and nothing more.

"Nah, I've worked around cattle too long to fear them. I think of it more like a healthy respect for the enemy." He laced his fingers through hers and gave them a reassuring squeeze, frowning when he realized how chilled they were. "You got a pair of gloves you can put on?"

She pulled away, tucking both hands around her saddle horn and ignoring his concern. "If this dredges up some bad memory, I can try to climb down there and cut him loose. I have wire-cutters in my bag."

"No way." He looked straight across at Jolene, then reached over and tucked her hair behind her ear, demanding her attention. His vow to keep his distance didn't apply when it came to protecting her and the baby. "I will ride on past and let that bull drown unless you promise me you'll stay at a safe distance with the horses."

"But he's unpredictable as it is. If he's hurt, there's no telling what he'll do. You'll need my help."

"I know what one of those creatures can do to a man. I know how he can tear your body—your whole life apart." Her knuckles turned white as she grasped the horn. He wanted to touch her again, to apologize for his harsh tone. But this was too serious to muddy his intentions with anything other than his words. "You can drive your truck fast, ride a horse through a hurricane, or hate my guts. But I will not budge on this."

"But it's too dangerous. What if we rope him and I tie him off on the saddle—"

"Jolene!" Her mouth snapped shut on a weak sigh. She looked so pale. Her shoulders sagged, and the unguarded moment of defeat revealed her fatigue. When she turned her head away, a shiver cascaded from her shoulders down through her hips and legs, shaking her hard enough to disturb Sonny beneath her. "Jolene?"

How long had she been running on pure bravado and willpower? *Screw this.* Nate pulled off his cap and plunked it on top of her head in an effort to conserve whatever body heat she had left. He leaned across his saddle, reaching for the blanket she'd tied behind her.

"We need to get you home. Get you warm and dry and get some food into you. You and the baby need to rest."

"No." She grabbed his wrist to stop his efforts. Her icy fingers held on with surprising strength. "Help Rocky if you can. Please. Not just for Lily, but for his sake. He's in pain and he's scared. I'll stay with the horses. I promise."

Those blue eyes were damn near impossible to resist. Nate quickly debated the merits of physical health versus mental anguish. But if he worked fast, he could help her with both. He looked deeply into her eyes, verifying her promise. She hadn't said anything she didn't mean yet.

But Nate was already breathing deeply, in through his nose, out through his mouth, slowing his pulse, clearing his mind, cinching his courage firmly into place. "You got a pen at your ranch that'll hold him?" Jolene nodded. "If I can fish him up out of that arroyo, we'll herd him to your place until this blows over. But once we get there, I'll take care of whatever needs to be handled. You change your clothes and get straight to bed. And we don't try to save anything or anybody else until Damon is gone. Understood?"

She nodded. Her fingers eased their grip ever so slightly so she could take his hand and squeeze it tight. "Thank you."

He raised her hand to his lips and kissed the soft, wet skin. "Don't thank me yet, angel."

He had to survive the rescue first.

His knee protested the climb to the ground. Judging by the stiffness, he had some major swelling going on. That knock on the dashboard, the twist in the ditch—as well as fatigue and weather—had definitely exacerbated the injury, which normally didn't give him such fits. But Nate gritted his teeth and bore the pain the way he did every other day of his life. He handed Checker's reins over to Jolene, pulled the wire-cutters from the saddle-bag and prayed.

Leaving Jolene and the horses a good twenty yards behind him, Nate limped toward the arroyo, speaking softly into the wind. "Easy, boy. I think you should know that I'm smarter than you. And if you work with me, I can help you."

Rocky spotted him halfway there and made another valiant effort to free himself.

Nate paused, propping his hands on his hips and shaking his head. "Now what did I tell you?" Other than twitching his cream-colored ears and snorting hot, steamy breath through his nostrils, the bull didn't move.

"You and I don't have to become friends, but we do need to cooperate." Nate moved closer, keeping his voice calm. "The little lady seems to think you deserve a hand, and I volunteered. That's what I do, you know. Volunteer. Help out where I'm needed." He was almost to the edge of the arroyo now. "To tell you the truth, you and the lady have a lot in common. Well, sure, she's a lot prettier than you are, and believe me, she smells a might better. But she's stubborn when it comes to letting somebody take care of her. Even when it's in her best interests and the man's willing to do it."

Rocky *had* been weakened by his effort to escape. He tried to spin around when Nate came too close, but the force of the water hit his flanks and nudged him back to the side of the ditch.

Allowing the bull a moment to get used to his proximity, Nate clipped the three wires away from the nearest fence post. He positioned himself to avoid the dangerous barbs that snapped back like a rubber band once he'd eliminated the tension from the lines. "See? That's a little better, isn't it? Now be patient and I'll get the other side."

Apparently the rapidly rising water had hidden a fence that dipped down into the arroyo and Rocky had either walked blindly into it or been swept against it. The rain had already loosened the sandy soil, and the bull had pulled a post from the bank, giving the lines just enough flexibility to entrap him.

Nate sniffed the air as he tried to figure out the safest way to approach the animal. About the only advantage he could see was that the wire had wound around Rocky's two left legs and caught on one horn, keeping the bull's head turned back toward his distinctive Brahman hump. He might be trussed up enough to keep him from goring Nate while he worked.

But Nate could still be crushed by the bull's weight, struck by a flailing hoof. And without a rodeo clown to distract the bull, once those horns were free, Nate would have to get himself out of there pronto, in case Rocky chose vengeance over freedom.

His decision made, Nate breathed in deeply, settling his nerves the way he used to do before dropping into the chute during his rodeo days. As quickly as he grounded himself, he knew he had to get things moving. The tang of salt in the wind stung his nose. It was the scent of the ocean—forty miles inland. It was Damon.

"I need you to set a good example for Jolene." Braced

for the worst and still hoping for a miracle, Nate waded in. His knee throbbed like a bad omen as he made his way down the uneven slope to the bottom. His back and thighs were getting sore, compensating for the pain. "Show how you can be strong and still accept a little common sense help from a friend. Of course, you might not like me any better than she does. Called me Solomon like I'm some old fart. But I'm her friend. I'm your friend, too. And whether you like it or not, I'm going to do this for you."

The cold water buffeted Nate's body from the chest down. His shoes were sinking into the muddy bottom. But he moved close enough to feel heat and smell the fear and panic emanating from Rocky's body. Keeping one eye on his half-ton nemesis, Nate reached beneath the water, gripped a wire between its barbs and snipped it as he spoke. "I don't expect you to thank me, I don't expect you to owe me anything in return. But please," he cut a second wire, "try not to hurt me any more than you have to. Surprisingly enough, I do feel pain."

Jolene's muffled shout sounded like a whisper in his ear over the slap of the water, the snorts of the bull and the roar of the wind. "Are you talking him to death or setting him free? You're using more words on him than you've said to me all day long."

Nate almost grinned. "See what I mean? So do me the favor?" He made another cut, freeing one leg. He dodged it as the bull kicked out. With room to maneuver now, Rocky hauled himself partway up the muddy bank. But…

"Ah, hell." Nate saw it coming. The current lifted him

off his feet and pushed him forward just as Rocky slid back into the water. One taut strand of wire still curled around the bull's horn, twisting his head back toward his shoulder.

Toward Nate.

Nate threw his arms back and kicked out, desperately trying to tread water and stop his forward momentum. He flipped over and tried to swim. But with a tool in his hand and a bum knee…

"Nate?"

Rocky bellowed. "Hell." Nate whirled around. If he timed this right, he could free Rocky and the bull would climb instead of charge.

Or Nate could wind up dead.

"Move it!" he shouted, startling the bull just as his hand snagged the wire. Rocky yanked, jerking Nate right up out of the water. The bull came down. Nate cut.

The wire snapped back as Rocky bolted free, the barbs tearing into Nate's shoulder and snagging his jaw. "Son of a bitch."

"Nate!"

Jolene screamed his name. It was the last thing he heard as the water surged around him and pulled him under.

"NATE!"

Before his coffee-dark hair disappeared under the water, Jolene had spurred her horse. With Checker in tow, she rode to the fence post closest to the arroyo, shouting at Rocky to keep him out of the water and away from Nate. Wherever he'd gone.

Had Rocky crushed him when he'd come down off the bank?

Had Nate's knee given out?

Was he drowning? Dead?

Her fear was a powerful stimulant, erasing cold and fatigue in a single heartbeat.

"Ee-yah!" She charged Sonny straight at the bull, turning him away from the arroyo. Nate's cap flew off her head and was lost. She pursued Rocky just long enough to ensure he'd lost interest in the man who'd saved his ornery hide. Once she was certain he'd keep trotting north along the fence line, Jolene spun around and galloped back to the water.

She'd dismounted and tied off both horses at the nearest fence post before she saw Nate surface again.

"Nate!"

"Damn wire." He cursed again, then dove back under. Or was he pulled?

Jolene shed her poncho and scrambled down into the ditch. Waist-deep, she grabbed her belly and shivered at the shock of cold water. "I'm sorry, baby. Be strong. Mommy has to help."

Nate spluttered to the surface again. His stern eyes locked on hers. "Get the hell out of here!"

Not gonna happen. "What's wrong?"

He sank before he could answer.

Jolene took a deep breath and dove into the rushing current.

A pair of strong arms latched on to her and dragged her to the surface. "Jolene."

Blood. On his face and neck.

"You're hurt."

Nate gasped for breath. "Get out."

The current hit them, splashed over their heads and

swept them under. Jolene kicked to the surface, pulling Nate with her.

"The wire-cutters." He spit water from his mouth, gulped down a quick breath. "I'm caught. Can't reach them."

He grabbed her arm and shook his head when she tried to dive down to retrieve them. The water was too murky, too fast. The bottom was washing away beneath their feet. She'd never find them.

But Jolene didn't know how to quit. She turned and half jogged, half swam toward shore. "There's another pair with the horses."

"Angel!" Whether it was a plea or a reprimand, she didn't stop to listen.

Jolene's legs felt like lead weights by the time she'd climbed onto solid land. The rain and wind were coming so hard at her, it was impossible to tell the difference between swimming and running. Her fingers worked like stiff, robotic appendages, but she finally got the saddlebag open, pulled out the wire snips and hauled ass back to the water.

"Nate?" She didn't see him. Couldn't hear him. "Nate?" She followed the path of the fence and stumbled into the water. A twinge of pain stabbed at the small of her back, but she ignored it. "Damn it, California, where are you?"

He was *not* going to leave her.

Just as quickly as her temper had flared and tears stung her eyes, Jolene rubbed her tummy. "Don't listen to me, sweetie. We're going to find him."

It was just enough comfort to keep her fighting.

"Nate?"

He popped to the surface, his bloody cheek the only thing visible as he spit and gurgled and got dragged back under. "Jo—"

Running on sheer determination, Jolene dove beneath the water. She swam into the wall of his chest. After a startling blind grab at her breast, he cinched an arm around her waist, snugging the baby between them. He anchored her to him while she ran her palm across his neck and torso, searching for the wire. He wrapped his free hand around her fist and guided the snips toward his shoulder.

His body jerked as she found the barbs embedded in his shoulder and chest. Her lungs burned for a breath of air. The muddy water chilled her to the bone. But time was running out. He held her; she worked. The screams inside Jolene's head were fading into a veil of fatigue and terror by the time she finally cut him loose.

She felt the sudden give as the trap released him. Opening her mouth in shock, she swallowed water. Nate's legs twisted with hers. Both arms came down around her and clutched her tight as he pushed off the bottom and thrust them both to the surface.

Jolene gasped for breath and coughed against the collar of his shirt. His chest heaved, crushing against her own as they fought to draw in oxygen from the water-soaked air.

"Oh, God, angel." His lips brushed against her temple, and his labored breaths rushed past her ear. "Oh, God… Are you with me?…The baby?…Talk to me… Are you all right?"

She was moving. But she wasn't aware of walking.

Nate was carrying her, tripping with her, dragging her out of the river and up the bank—crawling on his one good knee and pulling her along with him.

He was hurting. She was spent. His breath was little more than a hiss in her ear. But he kept going.

"Nate." She tried to find her feet, but they wouldn't function. They'd hit flat ground and he was still pulling her along with him. "Nate. Stop. Stop."

She bent her fingers into the shredded sleeve of his shirt and tugged. Or tripped him. She couldn't tell which.

All she knew was that she was sinking to the ground, shivering, exhausted, frightened for her baby and grateful to be alive.

Grateful Nate was alive.

Maybe not in one piece. But alive.

Nate collapsed behind her. His arms stayed around her and he cuddled her close. They lay in the mud, her bottom nestled in the curve of his groin. With one broad hand he cupped her belly, placing his fingers over hers, shielding the tiny life she carried inside her. With the other arm he provided a pillow for her head, and he rested his cheek against hers.

"Please tell me you and the baby are all right." Jolene only had enough energy to nod, but she moved her hand, sandwiching his larger one between both of hers. His chest expanded in a deep breath and his body relaxed against hers. His lips tickled her ear. Was he smiling? Did Nate Kellison really smile? "I thought I told you to stay with the horses."

Jolene's diaphragm shook with a silent laugh. "You're welcome."

"I owe you one."

He wrapped himself around her, offering her warmth and strength and thanks as the rain pelted down and the wind swept the world right past them.

CHAPTER SEVEN

"LILY?" Jolene had to practically shout into her cell phone to be heard through the staticky connection. "Can you still hear me?"

"Rocky's really okay?" her friend asked again.

Jolene picked up one of the towels she'd pulled from the linen closet and stuffed it into the windowsill beside her front door. Rain was already seeping in through every chink and hairline crack. Yesterday's sunshine and clear blue skies seemed like a figment of her imagination.

But she couldn't really stop to think about the gloom or the damp or the endless whistles and roars of the wind or else she'd drop from exhaustion. Her back ached and her bare feet were swollen like wrinkled prunes after being stuck inside her wet boots for so long.

She'd already started the water in the tub and pulled out all the pots and pitchers she could find so they'd have fresh water on hand in case the electricity went out and they lost the pumps, or rising floodwater contaminated the well.

While she prepped the house, Nate was taking care of the livestock and the outbuildings. That had been the deal, the only way she'd convinced him he didn't have to carry her into the house and tie her down to keep her from overextending herself again and possibly endangering little Joaquin.

Jolene's hand automatically went to her stomach, where Nate had shielded her and her baby from the elements. She'd mistakenly thought Nate was the strong, silent type. Of his strength, she had no question. He'd wrestled a bull, her, and the storm—and still had the temerity to boss her about.

But Nate had also made her laugh. He'd saved her life more than once today. He'd saved her friends. He'd held her in his arms and shared his heat and whispered soothing comforts in her ear.

And he'd kissed her like…like she was a woman.

Not Mitch Kannon's tomboyish daughter. Not Joaquin Angel's brave widow. Not April Kannon's plain, skinny little girl.

A desirable woman.

"Jolene?" Lily interrupted her thoughts. "Are you there?"

Jolene was hugging the towels so tightly, trying to hold on to the memory, that her arms ached. She quickly shook herself and stuffed another towel around the windows. "Rocky's fine. The horses, too."

If she'd had the energy to spare, Jolene might have grinned as she looked outside to the steel pen between the tall white barn and the tractor shed. The brown and white Santa Gertrudis bull, who'd nearly gotten them killed back at the arroyo, chomped on a mouthful of processed feed as Nate limped across the yard, leading Sonny and Checker into the barn for a quick, well-deserved rubdown. Her two dogs, Broody and Shasta, tagged along behind them, barking all the way.

That arrogant son-of-a-cow stood there and watched the parade, as lazy and content as if they'd chased him the last half mile across the prairie to visit a spa instead of saving his life and steering him to shelter from the hurricane.

"Don't worry, Lily. We'll keep him here at the Double J until after the storm. You're sure everyone's all right where you are? Did you hear from Gabe?"

"Yes. He's fine. He's so excited about having a little girl. He'll be staying at Mother's until there's an all-clear." Jolene barely listened to Lily's animated report. She was more focused on the dark-haired man whose knee was obviously giving him grief. The man who time and time again had put her needs and comforts before his own.

Jolene ached for his pain—the physical as well as the demons he tried to keep such a tight rein on. Someone needed to take care of Nate for a change. Tend his wounds inside and out.

Taking care of things was what Jolene did.

That stray puppy longing locked up her heart and made her yearn to fix his pain.

But *that* man? She cupped her tummy and felt something flutter, lower, beneath the baby. What could she really do for a man like Nate? A sexy, wounded, wise beyond his years man who stirred things inside her she'd never felt so intensely before?

She'd never been in love, not even with Joaquin. They'd been best friends and she cared deeply for him. But she'd never known this funny tightness around her heart before. She'd never felt flushed or excited just looking at a man—wondering what he'd say next, wondering when he'd touch her again. She'd never tasted passion before Nate Kellison had kissed her.

But she couldn't be falling in love with him. Uh-uh. No way. She'd known him for less than a day.

When he disappeared inside the barn, she was reminded that he'd be leaving once Hurricane Damon was said and done. Gone. Not a part of her life.

Jolene nodded, agreeing with the little voice inside her head that had guided her for so many years. *Nate's just here to do his job. He has no reason to stay. Doctor his cuts and bruises if you want. Fill his stomach with good food. But send him on his way before he hurts you. Before you hurt yourself by caring for someone else who's only going to leave.*

"Send him on his way," she whispered out loud. It would be the smart thing to do.

"What's that?" Lily yawned, or maybe it was a postpartum sigh. But the sound matched Jolene's somber mood. "Anyway, Amber is just so beautiful. So perfect. I wish I could reach Gabe again. I don't want him to miss a moment with his little girl."

"The phone lines must be down all over the place. I'm sure he'll call in as soon as he can."

"I hope so. What about you and Nate? Do you have the supplies you need to ride this one out?"

Jolene and Nate.

Don't even go there.

"We'll be just fine." Static clogged the line again. The winds must be going after the cell towers now, interrupting relays and cutting service. "Listen, Lily. I have to hang up. I need to call Dad while I still can."

"Thanks for everything, Jolene. I mean it. Everything."

Jolene disconnected the call, punched in her father's number and headed for the next window. Her home on the Double J was a true ranch house—a single-level, sprawling L-shaped stucco with four bedrooms and too many empty corners for one person to bang around in by herself.

Joaquin had been the only child of older parents who'd spent their lives building this place. He'd grown up working the ample spread and had inherited the rich cattle land upon his parents' death. But as the cancer made Joaquin sick and the bills mounted up, he'd sold off his herd and leased a portion of the land. Cattle still roamed the place, but they were someone else's responsibility. Jolene lived alone, with only her horse, Jericho, the dogs, and a collection of barn cats for company. She tended her garden, painted her baby's nursery, spoiled her father and wished she had more to do with her life.

Like take care of Nate Kellison.

"Damn it." Oh, Lordy, she was going to get hurt again if she didn't watch herself.

"Jolene? Criminy, honey, are you all right?" Mitch Kannon's gruff voice answered as soon as she'd cursed.

"I'm fine, Dad. Soaked to the bone and tired. But I'm okay."

"Where are you? I didn't think it'd take this long to hear from you. Is Kellison still with you?"

Jolene quickly gave him the details of their situation, along with the condition of the washed-out roads, broken fence lines and flooding. She mentioned Nate's injuries, their ride through the storm, and Rocky's rescue—though she left out the part about going into the river to cut Nate free. She reckoned there were some things an already worried father didn't need to know.

"How long do you think it'll be before it hits us, Dad?" she asked.

"It's only about a couple hours away now. The winds here are really picking up. We may have to evacuate to the school ourselves."

The sounds of raised voices in the fire station got louder. Jolene recognized Ruth Elliot's firm voice above all the others. "Mitch Kannon, get over here and drink this coffee while it's hot."

"Yes, ma'am."

Jolene smiled at her father's indulgent tone. He and Ruth had worked together for almost ten years. Ruth ran that office with the efficiency of a ship's captain, and though Mitch had often complained about Ruth's strict rules, he'd never once complained about the woman herself. In fact, he'd often mentioned how much he admired her. Hmm, Jolene wondered now. Was there something more going on between them?

Something her father had never given a chance— until confronted with doubts about their very survival.

A loud bang startled Jolene over the phone, and she heard a scream.

"Easy, Ruth." That was her father.

"Mitch, please." Was that a catch in Ruth's voice? "Come now."

"It's okay, Ruth. I'll be right there." Now *that* was the kind, firm voice that had reassured Jolene over the years.

Mitch's voice gained volume as he spoke directly into the phone again. "I've got to go now, honey. We just lost a window at the back of the station. We're moving everyone to the interior rooms until the worst blows over. I probably won't be able to contact you for a while." The connection crackled. "Eighty to one hundred mile per hour winds when it hits… Stay put where you are. Honey…" Static garbled the last of his message. Then the entire line went dead.

"Dad? Dad!" The cell tower must have been knocked out.

No radio. No phone. No contact with the outside world.

Only Jolene and Nate, an ornery bull—and Hurricane Damon poised to strike.

THE KNOCK AT THE DOOR startled her.

No one was out and about in this mess. Jolene dismissed the sound as something blowing against the house and went back to brushing her towel-dried hair and gathering it into a ponytail. She'd already changed into a dry pair of maternity jeans and zipped one of her dad's old sweatshirt jackets over a loose pink blouse that still fit her expanding figure.

After putting away her hairbrush in the medicine cabinet, she surveyed her handiwork. The small, interior bathroom off the master bedroom was probably the most insulated room of the house. Jolene had moved out the hamper and carried in sleeping bags, blankets, pillows, food and a couple of flashlights.

"Nesting instincts." Jolene was pleased with herself for seeing to their shelter *and* making herself slightly more presentable so that Nate wouldn't worry any more than he had to over her safety. Where was he, anyway? She hadn't seen him since they'd shared some leftover lasagna reheated in the microwave when they'd first arrived. Shouldn't he be hovering around her, telling her to stay put right about now?

The knock came again. Definitely the front door. Definitely not the wind.

With a sudden worry about a traveler who might have managed to strand himself in this weather, Jolene shut off the light and dashed through the house. "I'm coming!"

Padding across the cool parquet flooring in her bare feet, she swung open the front door and gaped in surprise. "Nate!"

She pushed open the screened storm door. "Why didn't you come on in?"

She retreated a step to let him enter, but he grabbed the screen, braced his arm against the jamb and didn't budge. Against a backdrop of charcoal gray sky and rain, he just stood there—a battered, bloodied warrior. Grim eyed and tight-lipped with fatigue and pain, he looked as if he'd barely escaped eight seconds of hell with a bull in the ring.

Jolene frowned. Besides the fact he was letting water blow into her foyer, she was annoyed with him for standing there and taking the beating from the wind and rain when he didn't have to. "California…"

He nodded at her use of the nickname, as if he'd expected it. "The horses are bedded down, and as far as I can tell, everything's secure. I saw that you have a spare room in the barn. I'm gonna bunk out there. I just wanted to make sure you were okay and tell you not to worry. I'll check in with you later."

She supposed the twisting movement of his lips in the middle of that five-o'clock shadow was supposed to be a reassuring smile. So he *had* had enough of her. He needed a break, some privacy. Or maybe he just didn't want her to see him suffer.

The first reason was a blow to her feminine pride. The second was an insult to her as a human being. Neither was a good enough excuse for him to lie on a cot in the barn when there were three perfectly good beds and a sofa in her house.

Jolene propped a hand on her hip. "That's ridiculous. There is plenty of space in this house. You can come in here and be warm and dry, and we'd never have to run into each other if that's what you want."

Nate narrowed his eyes. "I promised I wouldn't let things get personal between us. Out by that arroyo—I kind of forgot."

He was apologizing for something she'd been fantasizing about? Lordy, had she been on the wrong wavelength.

Jolene gripped the door and curled her toes into the growing puddle of water on the floor. "I guess...I forgot, too. I'm sorry if I made you uncomfortable."

Something in his eyes flickered, but then his face became a controlled mask once more. "So much has happened today, it feels like we've known each other a lot longer than we have. But it has only been one day. Your dad said you've been a widow for just a few months, and I've got some ghosts of my own, and we're just supposed to be together to work. To save lives. And animals and cars and trucks and things," he concluded with some of that deadpan humor.

But Jolene couldn't bring herself to smile. She'd lived through enough goodbyes in her life to know one when she heard it, no matter how noble the excuse. "So you're going to stay in the barn, in those wet, ratty clothes, with that gash on your shoulder. Now, is that because I'm in mourning and you think I can't handle having a man around, or because my dad wouldn't approve of us being together unless we're working?"

He released the door, not listening to any argument. "I'm staying in the barn."

Jolene stamped her foot as the screen door slammed. She shoved it back open. "Get in here."

Nate slowly turned and came back up onto the porch, standing almost chest to chest with her. He looked deep into her eyes, asking her to read the seriousness of his intent. "I gave my word to your father that I would keep you safe. From everything. I gave my word to you. If I come in, I might not be able to keep those promises. And I don't know if you're ready for that. I don't know if I am."

The rain splashed her face as she stared at him. Was she missing something here? Would another, more experienced woman be able to interpret the subtext of what he was saying? Turning him away went against every nurturing instinct she possessed. It went against every womanly desire she felt.

For Jolene, it wasn't that complicated a decision to make. The man needed her shelter; she needed his company.

She grabbed the front of his shirt and dragged him inside.

She let him drip on her floor while she closed and locked both doors.

Then she wrapped her arms around his waist, mindful of his wounded shoulder and startled catch of breath.

When his arms slowly folded around her back, she tucked her head beneath his chin and snuggled close.

"Stay."

"YOU'RE KILLING ME, woman. Ow!" Nate winced as Jolene dabbed antiseptic against the cut on his jaw. With his leg propped up on a cushion and an ice pack numbing his knee, he sat with his back against the arm of her denim sofa and let her treat every contusion and laceration she could find. Hell. He just hadn't realized how many there were and how thorough she could be.

"Hold still," she warned him as she applied a swab of liquid adhesive to the cut.

"You're killing me," he repeated. The sting burned through his shoulder next as she cut away the shreds of his T-shirt and poured a mixture of saline and alcohol into the five-inch gash from the barbed wire. He exhaled a deep breath and clenched his teeth to keep from jerking. "Literally."

"You're current on your tetanus, right?"

"Yeah." He'd had all his shots.

She peeled the stained cotton off his skin and tossed it on top of the pile of clothes that used to be his Courage Bay uniform. He'd transferred his keys and wallet and Grandpa Nate's ring into the baggy, split-kneed jeans she'd given him to change into. The rest of his things were headed for the Dumpster.

"Ooh. Um…Ooh." She caught her bottom lip between her teeth.

"That bad, huh?"

Her eyes darted skyward as the wind shook the roof over their heads, but it was the only indication that she was worried about the worsening weather. She still wasn't smiling when her gaze swept back over his chest. "You're going to need some stitches, at least where the barbs caught you. One gap's a half-inch wide, and the edges are pretty ragged."

Right. She was looking at the small picture, the wound, not the beat-up old man. He, on the other hand, had been studying the whole package—the fresh scent of her rain-washed hair when she leaned in close, the curve of her rump as she bent over to check her first-aid kit, the soft cadence of her voice as she grumbled over her supplies. The unintended thrust of her breasts as she straightened, then grabbed the small of her back and stretched, working out a kink there.

Sensual awareness suddenly gave way to concern. Nate reached around and laid his hand over hers. "Everything okay?"

"Just a twinge of back strain. The baby's fine." She pulled her hand away to cradle the swell of her belly. "He's been sleeping the past hour or so. I think he's tuckered out from everything he's done today."

"Everything his mother's done," Nate corrected, slipping his fingers beneath the hem of her gray sweatshirt and finding a knot of muscles at the base of her spine.

As he dug in and massaged the cramp through the fabric of her shirt, her chin came up and her eyes drifted shut as if she just might be enjoying his attentions. Her lips parted, and the contented sigh that escaped seemed to zing along every nerve ending in his body.

Definitely a boost to his ego.

He should have stayed in the barn. Away from the growing intimacy of a man and a woman cocooned in a warm shelter, trapped together by the storm outside. He should have ignored the sirenlike call of refuge he felt when he held her in his arms, and the welcome she offered with each tentative touch of her hands.

They'd endured so much today, grown so close. He felt as if they'd shared an entire lifetime already. Holding on to Jolene at the edge of that arroyo had been like holding onto a dream. Stripped of inhibitions by exhaustion and pain, he'd given in to the feelings she stirred in him. He'd held her as if she was his to hold, as if the baby she carried was his to cherish, as if saving each other's lives had bound them in some inexplicable way that no amount of time could ever change.

But those weren't the proper thoughts to have for a woman who was carrying another man's child, a woman who'd already loved and lost the man of her dreams. It wasn't right to think of what he wanted, when his job was supposed to be about protecting her.

He'd tried to leave her. But he'd gotten hauled in by her mulish Texas temper and seduced by the simple human need to hold on and connect with another person while the world went to hell all around them.

So instead of pulling away, he kept massaging her. He lifted up the hem of her blouse and slid his palm beneath. His fingertips found bare skin, warmer and softer than anything they'd touched before.

His own breathing quickened when she sighed with pleasure. "You like that, hmm?" he whispered, surprised to hear the deep-pitched huskiness of his voice. "Feels good to slow down sometimes, doesn't it."

They both started when the lights in the house flickered, following a show of electrical activity in the skies outside. The tension he'd eased immediately returned beneath his hand. Jolene pulled away, her mouth a grim line.

She tucked that long strand of hair behind her ear and got back to the business of tending his wounds. Nate took the hint. Hands off. Keep it casual. Her needs, not his.

"I don't think the liquid adhesive can hold the skin together on your shoulder," she reported in an efficient, apologetic tone. "It needs to be sutured."

"Do you do good work?"

She propped one hand on her hip and gestured with the other. "Nate, I don't have any anesthetic."

"You have a sterile needle and thread?"

"Yes, but—"

"Then stitch it up."

"It'll hurt."

Nate lifted his gaze to her compassionate one. *Get real.* He already felt like a piece of tenderized meat sitting here. What harm could a few stabs with a needle do?

It took one long visual sweep of all his cuts and bumps and bruises for her to get the picture. "Oh."

Besides, a little more pain might do the trick to suppress his desires for this beautiful woman.

A few minutes later, the lights were flickering almost nonstop. Nate held a flashlight and sat up as straight as he could while Jolene braced herself on one knee on the edge of the couch and stitched him together.

He winced as the needle pierced his skin, but he inhaled deeply and gritted his teeth to keep from jerking.

"Sorry." She apologized with the same breathy catch in her voice, the way she had after every other stitch.

"I'm okay."

For someone as dedicated to *relieving* pain as she

was, this had to be almost more torturous for her than it was for him. But to her credit, Jolene worked quickly and surely. One tear at the front of his shoulder had already been closed, and she was nearly done with the second one.

He felt the grating of the thread through raw skin. "Almost there." Another pinch. "Sorry."

The baby had awakened inside her to add his two cents to the world. Nate could feel a tickle of movement against his ribs as her belly pressed against him. This kid would have the same drive and energy as his mama, judging by the tiny, repetitive thrusts into Nate's flank.

Think clinical thoughts, he warned himself as he started to count each time he felt the flick of the baby's movement. "Try to remember that this will help me more in the long run. If the cut isn't treated now, it could get infected or refuse to heal."

"I know, but…" Tug. Wince.

"Ow."

"Sorry."

He barely felt the next prick of the needle. Clinical thoughts vanished. Jolene had shifted her position, lining up straight behind him to insert the last sutures at the jut of his shoulder. The tip of one perky breast poked his shoulder blade through the layers of material that separated them, and all of his senses careened and focused on that very spot. The whole breast pillowed as she leaned forward.

Nate swallowed hard. Her breasts weren't big, and she didn't accentuate them with the clothes she wore. But they were definitely there. And, like her personality, they had plenty of attitude. Despite his best intentions, that most masculine part of him couldn't help but take notice.

Maybe he should move the ice pack to his lap.

Prick. "Ow!" he cried.

"Sorry."

He'd been too preoccupied with female curves to feel that one coming. "Are you done yet?"

Her breast brushed across every sensitized nerve on his back as she got up to retrieve the first-aid kit. Nate's breath hissed between his teeth.

"It just needs a bandage," she said.

She reached over him to set gauze pads and tape on the back of the sofa. As she moved across him, her ponytail fell over her shoulder, stirring up the scent of rain-washed hair and traces of cinnamon and home-baked breads that still clung to her. Or maybe they just lingered in his imagination whenever she was this close.

"Jolene—" He couldn't come up with one clinical thought.

"Do you need a bandage anywhere else?" She pulled back and faced him. "I might let the other cuts breathe. As long as we can keep ourselves dry." With half a laugh, she smiled right in his face, offering him one of those dazzling wonders that made him think of long summer days and sunshine.

Nate tried to laugh, but an onslaught of emotions rose inside him, and the sound came out in a choked, heated gasp.

"I don't know…" She bent over at the waist to inspect the stitched-up wound. The front of her blouse gaped open, giving him a glimpse straight down to heaven.

Nate tried to look away, tried to blink. But he seemed to be a greedy son-of-a-gun when it came to Jolene's maternally enhanced figure.

"It's functional, but not very pretty," she observed.

"It's fine." Everything he could see was very fine.

"When we get back into Turning Point, I want that Dr. Sherwood friend of yours to take a look at it." Jolene probed the skin around her handiwork and Nate struggled not to wince. But goose bumps unrelated to pain prickled the instant she stroked her cool fingers across his heated skin, as if the caress hadn't been motivated by professional curiosity.

Jolene straightened to reach her supplies, hiding Nate's view of her cleavage, but she drifted even closer. Her thigh pressed against his and Nate groaned as inappropriate thoughts filled his imagination.

"Are you okay?" she asked.

Thank God he was beat up enough to camouflage the source of his pain. "Fine."

She cut lengths of tape and babbled on. "Hopefully, Dr. Sherwood has some dissolvable sutures she can replace these with. Otherwise, I'm afraid you're going to have a scar that looks like something Dr. Frankenstein pieced together."

Then she was smoothing gauze across the wound. Smoothing tape across his skin. Touching. Caressing. Pressing.

Nate gripped the back of the couch and the cushion beneath him, desperately trying to maintain some sort of distance. He could use a little help here. He might not be the most whole man on the planet. But he was still a man. The parts worked. The needs were there. She had the power to drive him nuts. He dipped his head, trying to connect his gaze to hers. "You do know what you're doing to me, don't you?"

Jolene pushed against his shoulder and stood bolt upright. Misunderstanding his question, she retreated a step in a noisy huff, her eyes sparkling with combat. "I might not have all the experience you do, but I am a trained volunteer. The only reason that cut doesn't look the best is because it was so ragged—"

"You have no idea, do you?" Nate frowned, his raging hormones on hold for the moment. She wasn't arguing the right topic. "I'm not talking about your medical skills."

"Then what are you accusing me of?"

"Nothing."

He thought he'd been teasing her, flirting, surviving. But she'd heard an accusation. It wasn't the first time he'd gotten the sense that Jolene wasn't as experienced as he would expect a married woman to be. Hadn't Mr. Angel ever had it so hot for his wife that he'd given her signals she couldn't miss?

Nate shifted to a more comfortable position, stretching his arms out to either side, inviting her perusal. "Do you notice anything at all about me?"

The light behind him flickered off, casting her into shadow. When it came back on, her cheeks were flushed with color. Her gaze danced over his chest, lingered on the obvious swelling in his jeans, and drifted back up to meet his unblinking eyes.

"Oh."

Now she understood.

He wasn't reading sympathy or even anger in her expression now. Confusion twisted her mouth. Despite the evidence that he was completely turned on by her, she still tried to dismiss the tension radiating between them as a medical problem.

"You're breathing faster." She picked up his wrist and pressed two fingers to the underside. "Your pulse is racing."

"Is yours?"

The sudden catch of her breath told him it was. She hadn't let go of him yet. "Do you need me to get you something?"

"No." Forget clinical thoughts and good intentions. He was a man on a mission, as serious as could be. Those blue eyes never broke contact with his, even as he reached for her. "This is what I need."

Nate pulled her into his lap, tunneled his fingers into her hair and fixed his eyes on her lips. "*You're* what I need."

He kissed her once, lightly, reverently. Her mouth remained still beneath his, and she braced one hand at the center of his chest to keep her distance. But there was something hopeful in her eyes, something sweetly nervous in that habitual tuck of her hair behind her ear. "But men don't—"

"This man does." The words seemed to shrink the air between them. She shivered, and the motion vibrated through his thighs and gathered in his swollen heat. He kissed her again. Her lips trembled this time, and her fingers curled into his chest. "This man wants you." He kissed her a third time. Her other hand joined the first. "Tell me no, you don't want this, and I will stop. I won't rush you into something you're not ready for." He fingered that silky strand of wayward hair himself. "But don't even think about questioning the way you've got my body primed to explode."

"That wouldn't be very nice of me."

"No, it wouldn't."

He cupped her cheek, savoring the soft, smooth curve. He traced the contour of her mouth with his thumb, then pressed into the lush fullness of her bottom lip. Her mouth opened in an evocative gasp, and moist heat blew across the tip of his thumb and skittered along every highly charged nerve ending.

"Are you going to listen to me this time?" he asked, zeroing in on that beautiful mouth. "Or do I need to keep talking?"

Now she was watching his mouth, and the wistful, wishful yearning in her eyes sapped the last of his patience.

He swallowed hard. "Jolene?"

"I don't know about talking."

She kneaded her hands against his chest, plucking loose a hair. Nate cringed at the nip of pain, suspecting it wouldn't be the last trial she'd inadvertently put him through before this day, this encounter, this assigned partnership was over. But he held himself still, waiting for some sign in those searching eyes that she'd made her decision. That she believed he found her sexy and attractive. That it was okay for a man like him to feel those urges for her.

Then her hands stilled, and her eyes met his. She smiled. "Wouldn't you rather just kiss me?"

Nate breathed a mammoth sigh. Normally he had the patience of Job running through his veins, but he'd really hoped he wouldn't have to go through with that talking part. "If you insist."

He thrust his fingers beneath her ponytail and pulled her in for a leisurely kiss. Her sweet, full lips blossomed beneath his gentle exploration.

"Mmm."

Her soft, contented sigh was music to his ears and a balm to his soul.

But Jolene Kannon-Angel had yet to grasp the whole *leisurely* concept. Whatever doubts she had about herself or his interest, she bulldozed her way past them. She threw her arms around his neck, knocked him back against the arm of the sofa and pulled herself right into his kiss.

"Whoa." Catching her around the waist, Nate shifted his balance to keep them from falling overboard.

"Too much?" Her arms stiffened. She frowned against his mouth.

The instant she began to retreat, he tightened his hold and pulled her squarely down on top of him.

"No. More than I expected."

Nate quickly got up to speed and joined her.

Reclining halfway, he smoothed his hand down her back, palming a handful of her bottom to align her lower body with his. He nipped at her lips, teasing, tasting. Their legs tangled together. And if her foot jarred his knee, he didn't care. Her hands were on his hair, her breath was in his mouth. And somehow she managed to get her hip nestled against his groin, protecting the baby from too much pressure and driving him crazy.

"Just right." He pulled the band from her ponytail and let her hair fall loose around his hands, over her shoulders. The silky tips brushed against his chest and tickled his jaw. "Absolutely right."

Nate kissed her—soundly, thoroughly. It was a

greedy affirmation of life, a reward for cheating death, an outpouring of passion and heart he'd never really allowed himself to tap into before.

And Jolene, bless her eager impulses, was there with him every step of the way. She kissed him back with her own untutored, uncensored, go-for-broke style he was learning to love.

She ran her palms across his beard stubble and giggled in delight. She followed the same path with her mouth. Her teeth closed around the jut of his chin.

"Is that okay?" she asked.

"Mmm."

"How's that?"

"Shut up, woman." She pulled one hand between them, skidding over his wound. "Ow."

"Sorry." Pushing herself up, she kissed the spot.

Her hand skimmed lower, catching a taut male nipple. Nate groaned at the lightning strike of pure pleasure that jolted through him. Misreading his agony, she shifted and kissed him there. "Angel," he protested, "you're killing me."

In the very best of ways.

Jolene's hands seemed to find every ache, every scrape. Her hot mouth and eager lips were there to apologize each time. She worked her way down his chest, dipped her tongue in his navel. Moaned and cooed and made him crazy.

It was the biggest adrenaline rush of Nate's life. More exciting than any bull ride, more thrilling than any ambulance call.

She eased the hurts of his body. Soothed the pain in his soul. Wakened his heart with unexpected hopes.

"Angel." He wanted to thank her. He needed her to understand even half of what she was doing to him. For him.

Nate gripped her by the shoulders and dragged her mouth back up to his. He rolled over, let her slide to the couch beside him. "This man…" He claimed her mouth. "Is definitely…" He unzipped her jacket, desperate to get inside to touch as much skin as she had. "Hot…" The buttons of her blouse went next. "For…" He twirled his tongue around hers, tasted the sweet hot temptation she offered. "You."

He slipped his hand inside her blouse and palmed her breast through its lacy cover. Her body jerked. "Nate," she whispered in that soft, sexy voice. He twirled the eager nipple between his fingers and thumb and she squirmed. "Nate." A heated gasp. He pushed aside the jacket, the shirt, the lace, and captured the straining peak in his mouth. "Nate!"

His name. Her voice. Adrenaline rush.

Her frantic fingers dug into his hair and held him against her as he laved the pert pink bud. Slipping his hand down to the swell of her belly, he gently cupped the proof of her utter femininity, all the while boldly savoring how masculine, how whole, how potent this woman made him feel.

He slipped his thigh between her legs. She clenched his hard muscles. Rubbed. Sought her own release.

"Nate? This is so good. I never… Please…"

He raised his mouth to reassure her with a kiss. "Easy, angel."

If she was this ready, this needy, he'd see this ride through to its conclusion. For Jolene, at least. He slipped his hand inside the elastic panel of her jeans. She whimpered as he nudged her through the damp crotch of her panties. She buried her face in his neck. Sighed. When he slipped one finger inside her, his own body jerked at her instant response. She was so tight. So hot. So ready. So—

A loud explosion ripped through the air outside, rattling every window in the house and plunging the room into darkness.

Nate wrapped her in his arms and pulled her tight against his chest.

Jolene screamed. "What was that?"

She snatched her hands away and tugged at her clothes, shoving Nate's sore shoulder as she scrambled up onto her knees. He cursed.

"Sorry."

She was apologizing? "Sounds like a transformer blew," he said.

"The electricity's out. I have candles and supplies in the bathroom."

Nate swung his legs to the floor. His knee and groin both protested the sudden movement. "Hell."

Lightning flashed, giving him a glimpse of Jolene zipping her jacket over her unbuttoned blouse and wiping the back of her hand across her mouth. Double hell.

He'd gone too far with her.

The bright light flashed long enough to leave him blind in the darkness that immediately followed. But he didn't need to see to know what a colossal mistake he'd made.

Seducing Jolene?

Playing around on the couch like a couple of teenagers discovering what sex was all about?

Sating his own selfish needs when it sounded like the whole state of Texas was blowing down around their ears?

I need a volunteer.
Keep my daughter safe.
Dead baby on the side of the road.

"Nate!"

Nate cursed. Every muscle in his body tensed as the pain of every failure, every lost chance buffeted him inside and out.

"Nate!" She latched on to his arm and shook him from his waking nightmare.

"I screwed up, Jolene."

"Screwed up what? You're Mr. Responsibility. You don't screw up. I must have done something wrong."

Lightning flashed. He saw blue eyes, wide as saucers. That need to rescue every lost soul was stamped on her face. *She* would rescue *him*. Crazy. He'd been too damn distracted to pay attention to how much danger they were in.

Some rescuer, some protector, some hell of a man he was.

The winds roared past, like an angry bull charging straight for them. No communication. No electricity.

Urgent fingers clung to him in the dark and begged for answers. "Nate, talk to me. What's wrong? Did I—?"

"You're fine! You're beautiful. Sexy—"

The front window blew out of its frame.

Nate grabbed Jolene and dove to the floor, covering her body with his as splinters of shattered glass flew across the room. A tidal wave of rain followed in its path, hitting them with the same fury as the flooded arroyo.

"What the hell is going on?" Jolene cried, burying her cheek in the rug beneath him.

Nate got to his feet, locked his arm around her waist

and scrambled for cover. In seconds he was closing the thick bathroom door and sinking onto a sleeping bag beside Jolene.

The whole house rattled on its foundation, reminding him of an earthquake. Dishes fell in the kitchen, crashed to the floor. Another window shattered. Nate tucked Jolene beneath his arms and shielded her as bits of plaster crumbled from the ceiling and rained down on top of them.

He had to shout to be heard.

"Damon's here."

CHAPTER EIGHT

THE ABSOLUTE QUIET finally woke her.

Jolene shoved her hair off her face and sat up, blinking her eyes against the dim light shining through the open door.

Feeling disoriented, she rubbed her tummy. "How did we sleep through a hurricane, sweetie?"

She was covered in a blanket, sitting on a pallet of open sleeping bags on the floor of the master bathroom. The hazy illumination was coming from a bedroom window. The generator must have kicked in, and the yard light had come on. It was bright enough to cast light, but no warmth. The eye of the storm had come.

And she was alone.

Nate had left her.

A sickeningly familiar feeling of abandonment washed over her, leaving her queasy and cold and fully awake.

Jolene glanced down. The collar of her misbuttoned blouse stuck out above the zipper of her faded jacket. Without a braid or ponytail to control it, her hair was a tangled mess. Of course, she had on no makeup. Her lips felt chapped. And she had to pee like nobody's business.

With such an attractive lump to wake up next to, no wonder Nate had skipped out.

With a resentful sigh, Jolene grabbed her flashlight, found her shoes and climbed to her feet. She'd bet good money her mother never woke up looking anything but drop-dead gorgeous. She poured a cup of water from one of the bottles and rinsed her mouth, ran a brush through her hair and put her clothes on right. Of course, she could bet equally good money that her mother would never allow herself to be caught in the middle of a hurricane or any other natural disaster.

That's when she smelled the rich aroma of spices and charcoal in the air. "What the heck?"

Jolene ventured out of the john and followed her nose outside. She swept her light past the devastation in her living room—shattered glass and leaves sprinkled liberally over every piece of soaking wet furniture, splintered frames from the windows gouging out chunks of her prized wood floors, the branch of an old scrub pine, stripped of needles and lying in front of her television console.

The kitchen had been hit, too. Piles of broken dishes had been swept into the corner by the trash can. Her fridge and freezer stood open, empty and dark, while the contents had been packed into a cooler with ice or stacked neatly on her island countertop.

Jolene continued massaging her tummy at the odd sight. "I don't think the hurricane picked up after itself."

Nate.

She refused to pay mind to that little flurry of hope that quickened her pulse. Maybe Nate hadn't left her behind so much as he'd gone on to do something else.

"Nate?" Jolene pushed open the back door and went outside. The ominous silence in the air spooked her more than the constant bombardment of the storm had. After finding a secluded spot to relieve herself, she headed around to the front and stared at disaster. The circle of illumination cast by the yard light revealed a world of chaos in the place she called home. Beyond the fringes of light, there was nothing but blackness and the threat of Mother Nature lying in wait to do even more damage.

"Oh, my God."

"It's not as bad as it looks."

Nate's calm voice called to her from across the yard, where he was pulling out broken limbs and chunks of wood from the corner of Rocky's pen. She aimed the beam of her flashlight at his reassuring presence.

Jolene's first thought was that her father's jeans were too big for Nate's slim hips, and Joaquin's white T-shirt was too small for Nate's more muscular frame. Her second thought, the one that made her swallow hard and say a grateful prayer, was that she was just plain glad to see him.

Maybe a little too glad, she cautioned herself.

That tight white shirt showed every flex of muscle as he worked. She couldn't resist watching him move, his limp minimized by the power and precision that defined the rest of his body. Even bruised and battered, she'd found that body an irresistible treasure to explore. But for now, maybe forever, she'd have to content herself with just looking.

Tucking away any yearnings or regrets that lingered from almost making love for the first time on her couch, Jolene concentrated on safer feelings, like the security she'd felt when he'd held her in his arms during the worst of the storm.

"If this is *good,* I sure don't want to see *bad,*" she answered at last. "You should have gotten me up. I would have helped."

"It's the middle of the night. You needed your rest. I needed some fresh, dry air." And some distance from her?

Jolene crossed the yard, picking up pieces of trash along the way. "What is it now, about one o'clock in the morning?"

"A little after."

Maybe hunger accounted for the uneasy feeling that lingered in her stomach. She could hope it was that simple and not a symptom of confused feelings or thwarted lust. "Have you had a chance to assess the damage?"

Broody, her lab retriever, and Shasta, a pint-size terrier mix, darted in and out of the shadows around Nate's feet, guarding the place, supervising his work, checking out anything interesting that crossed their path. Seemed they'd adopted their California guest much more quickly and easily than she had.

Nate scratched Shasta behind the ears, then tossed a stick for Broody to fetch. The big dog gladly bounded off into the darkness. Seemed as if Nate had no problem dealing with them, either.

Just their owner.

"Not too much beyond the obvious," Nate told her. "The animals are all accounted for, though." He shooed Shasta away from the bull's pen. "Even Mr. Stud here seems to be doing all right for himself."

Bits of debris clung to Rocky's hide, but there were no visible signs of injury beyond the cuts he'd sustained from the barbed wire. The bull chewed on the leafy end of a branch that had blown into his pen. He had the gall to stare accusingly at Nate, as if the storm had interfered with his wanderlust and somehow the humans were to blame for the inconvenience.

"Lily shouldn't have worried," Jolene said. "I'm not sure anything can kill that bull." If only the rest of her property could be so tough. She slowly turned with her light, taking stock of the destruction.

The tractor shed was little more than a pile of twisted metal siding wrapped around the tractor and old beater truck that had been parked inside. Shingles from the barn roof were scattered across the ground. And there was debris everywhere. Leaves, branches, tumbleweeds, items she couldn't identify. What looked like a little girl's dollhouse sat in the pile of trash Nate was stacking beside the barn.

Jolene walked over and inspected the toy's mud-stained interior. "I wonder where this blew in from. Someone's going to be missing it."

"I hope the girl it belongs to is in better shape. That her mother got her down into a basement or took her to a public shelter." Nate tossed an armload of loose planks onto the pile and went back for another load.

"I'm sure she's fine."

"Yeah." He didn't sound convinced.

What was it that caused him such pain? She suspected it went far beyond ripped-up skin or a shattered knee. But if he didn't want to confide in her, she wasn't going to ask. As much as she'd loved that teasing, talkative, passionate side of Nate, she sensed that he needed to reassert his self-control in order to cope.

Though whether he was coping with the past or the present, survival or regret or her, she had no idea.

"Can't this wait 'til morning?" She picked up some downed branches and added them to the pile. Keeping busy seemed to distract them both from uncomfortable thoughts. "I'm assuming that's your work in the kitchen, too?"

"I wanted to make sure Rocky was secure and the generators were working. Since we don't know how long we'll have to conserve electricity, I thought we'd better do something with the food before it went bad."

But spoiled food wasn't her primary concern. She thought of her father and the hundreds of evacuees he was responsible for. If Turning Point had been hit like the Double J, Mitch Kannon would need every volunteer he could get to help out. "You don't think power and communication will be established anytime soon?"

Nate shook his head. "I doubt it. And with power out, roads flooded and communication down, I doubt anyone's looking for us yet, either."

Jolene dumped her load. "So it's just you and me for a while longer, huh?"

"Looks that way."

Adam and Eve, stranded in a weather-beaten version of Paradise. Only Adam was brooding and distant and Eve didn't know how to handle a man who wasn't her father, friend or patient.

Jolene suddenly felt edgy and uncomfortable as she recalled in vivid detail every sweep of Nate's hands, every claim of his mouth on her body, every delicious word they'd shared on the couch before the hurricane hit. Her breasts beaded into painful nubs, her lips tingled, and the female heart of her grew heavy and damp between her legs.

She braced her hand against the side of the barn and clutched at her belly. Her breath came in ragged gasps. Squeezing her eyes shut, she tried to regain control of her body's raging hormones. She'd never... No man had ever... And, God, she'd wanted him to finish. She'd wanted...

"Jolene?" Nate's concerned voice cut through her wanton thoughts.

No teasing voice, no soft seduction.

He'd come up right behind her. She could feel the heat from his body, though he didn't touch her. She turned, still clutching her stomach, feeling light-headed and pale. Thankfully, Nate was a paramedic, not a mind reader.

"Are you hungry? I know you and the baby need to eat regularly." Oh, yes. Very practical. Very Nate. "I fired up your propane grill in the garage and I'm cooking some steak and eggs for a late-night snack."

That would explain the yummy smell she'd detected earlier.

Jolene forced herself to slowly exhale.

Hungry? Yes. Though not necessarily for food. But she could never admit that.

Fixing a smile on her face, she glanced up into those serious brown eyes.

"Are you kidding?" she said. "I've been hungry for the past five months."

JOLENE WANTED TO COVER her ears and scream. The pounding of the rain and wind had been relentless for the past few hours.

Just as her father had told her, the back wall of the hurricane was even more powerful than the outer bands or front wall had been. The rain still fell, insulating them inside the house. And though they had no official report to go by, she suspected the wind could be clocked upwards of one hundred miles per hour. The bathroom was shrouded in darkness, save for the candles she'd lit.

But even candleglow couldn't dispel the tension gnawing at her. She must have been transmitting her restless energy because Nate leaned down from his seat on the edge of the tub and slid a tray with some of the snacks she brought in earlier across the sleeping bag to where she sat on the floor, leaning against the door.

"Here. You haven't tried dessert yet. A pudding cup or applesauce?"

Jolene gave a nervous laugh. "It's hard to think about eating in the middle of a hurricane."

"My grandpa Nate believed the best thing to do in a crisis was eat. He also loved desserts and thought they should be served at the beginning of the meal."

She peeled off the pudding container, picked up a spoon and took a bite. "I think your Grandpa Nate was a very wise man. Are you named after him?"

He nodded. "My older brother, Robert, was already named after my dad. Grandpa was our only other living male relative. Family tradition."

"So you were close?"

"He raised us until I was twelve." He read the curious question in her arched brows and answered it matter-of-factly. "My parents died in a car crash when I was one. So we went to live on Grandpa Nate's ranch. He was the only parent I ever really knew. I was twelve when he died. My brother, Kell, was eighteen and legal by then, so he, Jackie and I stayed together and just sort of took care of each other."

The fact that he'd glossed over the difficult childhood he and his siblings must have had, went a long way toward explaining those *life* things he kept under such strict control. Jolene's throat constricted as she worked to control some feelings of her own. Her compassionate heart thumped loudly enough in her chest that she wondered if Nate could hear it over the storm.

"I'm sorry about your folks and your grandpa. That must have been hard on your brother, having a family to take care of at that age."

Nate scooped out the last of his own pudding cup and shrugged as if there was nothing remarkable about his family's story. "Kell was going through some personal stuff, just out of high school, trying to be in love and make his place in the world. He gave up a lot for us. Always made sure there was a roof over our heads and somebody to answer to. Jackie and I were still in school, but we held down the homefront. Turned myself into a pretty good cook and ranch hand."

Watching him double-check the flashlight batteries and drinking water supply, Jolene got the feeling that Nate had done a lot more than cook meals to help his family.

"Sounds like you and your brother and sister are as close as Dad and I are."

Nate propped some pillows against the tub and settled onto the floor opposite Jolene. "It's easy to see that Mitch adores you."

"It's mutual, believe me." Just mentioning her father

and the deep bond they shared helped Jolene tune out the storm.

Damon's dramatic arrival had kept Jolene from thinking about how close she and Nate had come to making love, and talking with Nate these past few hours had dispelled any awkwardness she might have felt. Nate had shared enough about his past to help her understand that grave sense of responsibility he carried on his shoulders. But now she chose a more neutral subject. "Tell me about California. All I know is that's where my mother lives now, with some Hollywood exec type."

She nearly choked on her next bite of pudding. Had she actually said that out loud? She'd wanted to keep Nate talking, not delve into her own past.

Nate was nothing if not observant. "Is that what you've got against California? Your mom? Your stepdad?"

"Stepdad number two." Jolene laughed, but there was no humor involved. "Anyway, the dad part implies that they're somehow a part of my life. They're not. Mom left Dad when I was eight. She never looked back. She said she wasn't cut out for family life or small towns or boring people. The bright lights of Hollywood were much more appealing than a little tomboy and a salt-of-the-earth hero. She didn't want us anymore, so she left."

"Ouch."

"Big ouch."

"So Mitch raised you on his own?"

Jolene nodded.

"He did a good job," Nate said.

She heard the compliment, but didn't acknowledge it. "That might explain why I'm a little lacking in the fashion sense and sex appeal department. But I can change my own tires and play a mean third base."

Nate repeated himself. "He did a good job."

Jolene curled her legs beneath her, pretzel-style, and pulled a pillow into her lap. It gave her antsy fingers something to play with, gave her something to hide behind. Nate watched every self-conscious movement, but made no comment. And she didn't offer anything more. Thinking about her mother left her feeling as raw and battered as the world outside. "I don't want to talk about me. Tell me about Courage Bay and your ranch."

After a lengthy pause, Nate took a deep breath and told his story. "Grandpa Nate named the ranch Whispering Dawn. We raise quarter horses there. Actually it's in the mountains outside of town. Hills. Trees. A lot greener than this. Courage Bay itself is right on the ocean, on about a ten-mile stretch of white sand beach. It has a small-town feeling for a city, and though we're not that far from L.A., we're definitely not Hollywood."

"Sounds beautiful." Sounded like he missed it.

He talked about their registered AQHA horses and his brother's and sister's recent weddings. He told her the story about a crew of shipwrecked sailors during the Mexican War and the Native Americans whose heroic rescue had given Courage Bay its name. He talked about his buddies at the fire department and the recent crime wave involving a serial bomber nicknamed the "Trigger," who had terrorized the city. When the culprit had finally been exposed, he turned out to be the fire department's mechanic, a man Nate had once considered a friend.

Gradually Jolene relaxed. The even cadence of his

deep voice was doing the trick. The storm faded into tolerable background noise as the world shrank down to this tiny, insulated room and the man she shared it with. He was a sexy, wounded crusader who had left behind the world he so obviously loved to save her friends, help her dad, keep her safe and sane, and protect her baby.

Because that's what a man like Nate Kellison did.

Jolene decided that she liked Nate Kellison. Liked him very much.

"Have you ever actually been surfing?" she asked, embarrassed now to think of the way she'd stereotyped this California cowboy as some kind of know-it-all, life-in-the-fast-lane surfer dude.

He picked up her empty pudding cup and tossed it with the dirty dishes beneath the sink. Then he settled against the bank of pillows in front of the tub to stretch out his leg and rub his knee. "A few times. Back in high school. But I got enough thrills competing in the rodeo. Once you conquer a bull like Rocky, who needs the ocean?"

Watching his fingers work reminded her of the massage he'd given her. The gentle strength of those fingers had erased the cramp in the small of her back and worked other types of magic on her body, too.

But just as Jolene was succumbing to the languid warmth of his soothing voice and the fiery memories of how incredibly sexy and alive he'd made her feel, a loud pop startled her and brought the outside world back into their cocooned retreat. Another tree branch had fallen prey to the storm. Jolene squeezed the pillow in her arms, anxious to resume the conversation and keep the tension of the hurricane at bay.

"So you were conquering a bull like Rocky when you got hurt?"

Nate nodded. "Bull-riding was my specialty. I earned a rodeo scholarship that put me through college. My junior year, at the regional championships, I drew a monster called Tornado. He had a good five hundred pounds on Rocky out there."

His fingers stilled, and he paused long enough that Jolene inched forward, wondering if he would continue.

"I lasted seven seconds on his back," he said at last.

Jolene drew back at the bleak announcement. "I thought you had to ride for eight seconds to qualify."

Nate raised his eyes to hers. "That's right. By eight I was flying through the air. Probably blew out my knee when I hit the dirt." He shook his head and leaned back. "I don't remember much after that. I had a concussion, too."

"Nate." She rose up on her knees and clasped his ankle because that was the only part of him she could reach to offer comfort. To find some for herself.

"Kell was there in the stands. He said Tornado came after me like there was something personal between us. And I was locked up against the fence."

Jolene felt moisture prick her eyes.

"Anything on me that hadn't been broken yet sure was on that day," Nate continued. "I'd already had the first of four surgeries by the time I could think straight and figure out where I was. I lost part of my knee. The doctors have gradually rebuilt my leg with steel pins and replacement parts. Needless to say, I was done with the rodeo. Kept my hand in it at the ranch, but that was about it. I'm fit enough to pass a physical, but not much more." He laughed, but Jolene couldn't feel any humor. "Now it takes an extra hour to get me through the airport. And my leg makes a pretty effective paperweight."

A tear trickled down Jolene's cheek and dripped onto the back of her hand. She felt just as hot, just as small and useless as that tiny drop in the face of all Nate had endured. "Nate, I…"

Jolene swallowed hard. She didn't know what to say. *I'm sorry* seemed inadequate. *Poor thing* seemed an insult to the strong, capable man he'd become in spite of his tragic past. *Let me hold you and comfort you and give you something of me to make you feel better* seemed downright laughable, given her lack of experience with men.

Nate reached out and caught the next teardrop with the pad of his finger. "Hey. I'm not telling stories to bring you down. You were supposed to at least smile at that last one."

His touch was sure and gentle, and the selfless caress made her weep all the more. "You're not very funny."

"Jolene, don't do this."

She was making things worse, not better. She could tell by the deep worry grooves that formed beside the grim line of his mouth.

"C'mon, angel," he urged her.

Jolene gave a noisy sniff and pulled away. "I'm sorry. I'm just tired. And my hormones are all out of whack. And this stupid storm won't stop." Sitting on her legs, she hugged herself—baby, pillow and all—sat up straight and did her very best to glare through her soggy vision. "But that's not why I'm upset. You act like you're tough and in control, but you're in pain all the time, aren't you:"

"It's not that bad—"

"You take care of your family. You rescue drowning bulls and flaky blondes, and deliver babies. You—"

"Jolene—"

Anger and guilt blended with compassion. "My baby and me—we're an extra burden you've decided to take on for the duration of your trip to Texas."

"Your father asked me to keep an eye on you."

"You don't have to." She hadn't survived twenty years without a mother or a man of her own without developing a few coping skills. Sure, she'd gotten into plenty of scrapes. But that was human. She'd gotten herself out of just as many. Why couldn't he see that? "Every father worries. But I'm twenty-eight years old. And you're not my dad." Not in any way, shape or form. Not with everything those broad shoulders and tight buns and controlled sense of duty stirred inside her. "You have enough to deal with already. You don't have to protect me."

Nate bent his good knee and leaned forward to prop his elbow against it. "Somebody sure needs to. You're so busy taking care of everyone else, you don't take proper care of yourself or your baby."

"We've done just fine on our own, thank you very much. Joaquin, Jr., is as healthy as he should be. *I'm* as healthy as I should be." She angled her head, pointing to the hole in his jeans that revealed his scarred, swollen knee, and to the shoulder bandage that showed through his white T-shirt. "You're the one who's trying to take on too much."

"I am not an invalid," Nate said, articulating every word. "I can handle whatever I have to. That includes you…and the baby."

Jolene's defensive anger evaporated on her next breath. The conversation stopped, and the room fell silent.

"You have to keep the baby safe." There was raw emotion in the command and it pierced Jolene's womanly heart. Then Nate blinked and turned his face away, severing the contact.

The baby again. What was it about children and babies that haunted him so? That turned him into Attila the Protector? She splayed her fingers across her belly, bracing herself, shielding her little one from whatever horrid truth tortured this man.

"What happened with the baby, Nate?" she whispered, needing to know. There was such loss, so much grief, so much defeat in his voice.

But Nate was done talking. She could see it in the controlled set of his face. Jolene hugged herself around the pillow and let the tears roll down her cheeks.

"Ah, hell." With that much of a warning, he reached out, snagged her by her shoulders and drew her up across his body and into his arms. He tossed the pillow aside and snuggled her down onto the floor beside him so that they lay together, chest to chest, heat to heat. His grip was hard, his body strung tight as a lasso with a running calf caught in its noose.

But the strong, steady beat of his heart soothed her ear. And the warmth of his body seeped into hers.

He nestled her head beneath his chin and rubbed slow, easy circles at her nape. Jolene could only wrap her arms around his waist and hold on and cry. He didn't explain anything. But countless moments later, she felt the tension inside him break. Felt it in the deep sigh as his chest rose and fell. Then his whole being relaxed.

"Hey, those better not be for me," he said. "I'm okay." His low-pitched voice rumbled deep as he pushed the hair back from her face. But something had let go inside Jolene, too, and she couldn't seem to stop crying. He tipped her chin and marked the trails of her tears with the callused pad of his thumb. "C'mon, angel. I don't have any cure for this in the first-aid kit."

She swiped at her eyes with the back of her hand. "I'm sorry. It's those pesky hormones." And fatigue. And the deep, abiding hurt she felt for Nate's suffering, despite his assertion that he was okay.

It was frightening to realize that she'd grown closer to this man in one day than she'd been with her own husband after one year of marriage.

Jolene freed her chin and snuggled back against him. They simply held each other. Beyond her father's loving bear hugs, she'd never been held so securely, so tenderly by any man. She'd never felt the comfort, the belonging, the possessive sense of rightness that she felt in Nate Kellison's arms.

She hugged him close and tried to give him back everything that he made her feel.

The winds blew and the storm raged and Jolene never budged from her secure haven.

"So tell me about Turning Point," Nate asked, stroking his fingers up and down the back of her neck. "Where'd you get a name like that?"

Jolene had closed her eyes to savor his touch. Now she grinned in drowsy contentment. "The story goes back more than a century ago. A wagon train of immigrants was traveling south through Texas—looking for a new life in the promised land. Fertile ground, oil underneath. Freedom."

"The people of Turning Point seem pretty resourceful," Nate commented. "I can believe that you come from pioneer stock."

"Germans, English, Irish, Scandinavians, Czechs and Poles. But they weren't as friendly then as we are now. They quarreled often and had trouble communicating because of all their different languages and customs."

"You're not going to tell me this ended in some kind of massacre, are you?"

"No." Jolene shrugged. "But at the rate they were going, it didn't look too much like they were going to make it to any promised land, either." She shifted position as the baby stirred between them.

"Hey. I felt that." The awe in Nate's voice reverberated through the tiny room and settled deep in Jolene's heart.

"You want to feel him?"

"Do you mind?" She heard something almost like fear along with the excitement in his voice. Though she couldn't guess the cause, Jolene sensed that this was a healing moment for Nate.

And she desperately wanted to share the joy of this pregnancy with someone who could see it as a miracle instead of a poorly-timed lab experiment. She took Nate's hand and spread it flat on her belly, beneath the hem of her sweatshirt. "He's just a flutter right now. A swish of movement when he changes positions. He doesn't really give a good kick yet."

But little Joaquin delivered, rolling over, almost thrusting himself into the warmth of Nate's hand.

Nate's breath caught. "Wow."

Wow was right. Jolene laughed at Nate's unexpectedly boyish delight. "He likes you."

Nate moved his hand to follow the movement of the baby. "Does he do that all the time?"

Slipping her hand down to cover Nate's and hold him against her as the baby quieted, Jolene smiled. "Only when he's in the mood. See? He's settling down already."

"He likes to hear you talk. Your voice is so—"

"Annoying? Never-ending? Opinion—?"

"Soothing." He cut her off and complimented her at the same time. "That soft, throaty whisper gets to me, too. It's sexy. Like something secret and intimate that only two people are supposed to share."

Jolene's cheeks heated with embarrassment. She'd been called skinny, shapeless, fun, crazy, plain, understanding and a real pal by the men in her life. But never soothing. Never sexy.

Embarrassment gradually turned into something much more profound, something that nurtured her ego and gave her confidence and made her feel pretty. "I think that's the sweetest thing any man's ever said to me. Thanks."

"Sweet? Yeah, now that's what I was going for." He slid his hand down and gave her rump a playful swat. "The smooth talkin's done for the night, angel. Now go on. Finish your story."

Jolene laid her head on his chest and snuggled in. "The only thing holding all those immigrants together was their determined wagon train master, William Wallace Livesay. He could speak enough of each language to communicate with all the groups and keep the peace.

"But he was killed when a storm a lot like this one hit. He was thrown from his horse and trampled. The settlers were suddenly on their own, stuck with each other. But in true Texas spirit, they turned their lives around and decided to work together and settle at the spot where their leader had died. They found a way to communicate, a way to get along. They turned away from the storm and to each other to survive."

"They turned to each other to survive," Nate echoed.

"Sounds familiar, doesn't it?"

She and Nate had turned to each other.

"Sounds like that pioneer spirit—putting down roots, helping your neighbor, doing what needs to be done—is still a big part of Turning Point."

"I guess so. Is it like that for you back in Courage Bay?"

He didn't answer. Maybe he was feeling torn from his own roots. From the community and family he loved back in California.

"It's quieting down out there," he pointed out after a long silence.

Jolene turned her head to listen. She'd been so caught up in her time with Nate—that she'd momentarily forgotten about the wrath of Damon blowing its way across the countryside. She could still hear the rain hitting the roof, but she no longer felt the wind pummeling the house or roaring through the rafters. The air pressure had changed, too. Maybe it was only psychological, but she sensed the atmosphere lightening up, easing its hold over the elements.

And in direct contrast, Jolene's heart grew heavy. Maybe it was just exhaustion. Nate was putting her to sleep, massaging the back of her neck with one hand. And maybe it was something more. She'd run a gamut of emotions today, but one remained, startlingly clear.

She liked Nate Kellison. A lot. She wanted him. Needed him. He'd awakened both her heart and her body.

And there'd be no reason for him to stay once the storm had passed.

"You okay?" he asked, misinterpreting her silence.

Jolene snuggled closer, postponing the inevitable. "You really do have magic hands, Nate Kellison."

She drifted off to sleep, secure against the warmth of Nate's broad chest. Little Joaquin settled, too, equally at home beneath the large, gentle hand of the California cowboy who had melted his mother's heart

And would surely break it when he left her to go back home.

CHAPTER NINE

THE SUNSHINE HURT his eyes.

Nate squinted against the morning light and surveyed what was left of the Double J ranch. Most notably, he assessed the bull pen. A chunk of Jolene's barn roof was lying across a section of demolished fence rail, and there was no bull in sight. Branches and fences were damaged or down everywhere. A lake, left by Damon flooded the lowlands off to the west, and the road beyond the Double J's main gate was nonexistent beneath a wash of mud and standing water.

When Texas staged a disaster, they did it up right. After everything he'd seen the past twenty-four hours, he'd been ready to think the sun never shone in this part of the country.

Jolene walked up behind him on the front porch. "Oh, this is not good."

Nate quickly amended his opinion on Texas sunshine. He'd never failed to see it in the beautiful smile of one spunky, blue-eyed mom-to-be.

"Not good at all," he agreed. His mood seemed to lighten just by having her stand beside him. "It's hard to know where to start cleaning up."

She wore clothes today that emphasized her slender

height and actually showed off a bit of her figure, and
had pulled her hair back into one long braid that high-
lighted the graceful column of her neck. Maternity jeans
hugged her rump and thighs. She'd left the bottom button of her royal blue tailored blouse unfastened to ac-
commodate her protruding belly. With her arms crossed
in front of her, pushing her breasts up, she created a lush
silhouette of femininity that stirred a decidedly masculine response in him.

How could she ever think a man couldn't find her attractive? Wouldn't want to kiss her? Wouldn't move
heaven and earth to make love to her?

Not for the first time, Nate wondered about Jolene's
relationship with her husband. He only knew that the
man had been sick and had tragically died before the
two of them could enjoy creating a life and future together. But what about before that? Had her husband
courted her? Sent her flowers? Said pretty things? Or
had he just taken advantage of Jolene's bighearted instincts to give of herself without regard for herself? It
burned in Nate's gut to think that this Joaquin Angel had
had sex with Jolene, yet not shown her the joys of making love.

Hell. His gut wasn't thrilled with the idea of anyone
making love to Jolene. Well, anyone but him.

Squeezing his eyes shut, Nate turned his face to the
sky. He had no business feeling possessive or jealous or
resentful about any of this. Jolene wasn't his. Judging
the way her husband had loved her wasn't his concern.

"I feel like we're surrounded by a medieval moat."

Jolene's take on the condition of her ranch rightly
pulled him back to less personal thoughts.

"You don't happen to have a drawbridge you can let down to get us out of here, do you?" she asked.

"Not on me." Nate checked one of the porch's posts before leaning against it. "If the Agua Dulce's flooded to the south, then every slough and tributary feeding into it is backed up, too. It could take a day or a week for the water to go down enough to walk or ride out of here."

"If we had a boat, I'd say we could paddle."

Nate turned her way. "Do you have a boat?" Maybe there was a way he could get beyond the barriers of floodwater and find help after all.

Jolene shrugged. "Sorry. Looks like you're stuck with me."

He could think of worse ways to spend the next few days of his life.

"I'm not complaining." Nate straightened, pulling his gloves from the pockets of his jeans. "There's plenty of work I can do around here." He pointed across the rain-pocked yard. "And that ton of trouble is my first priority."

Jolene stared at the empty, broken pen. She twirled a finger in the air as she spoke. "You don't think the hurricane spawned a tornado…that Rocky…" He could tell she was imagining what she'd have to report to her friend, Lily, if the Santa Gertrudis bull turned up dead. "The cows blew away in the movie *Twister*."

Shaking his head, Nate grinned. "Now *that's* Hollywood. But I suppose anything's possible. Knowing our friend, though, I'm guessing he took himself for a walk at the first opportunity. He's probably trying to find your neighbor's herd or some dry food."

"Or he's lying in wait for us somewhere."

"I wouldn't put it past him." He pulled out his work

gloves. "Better keep your eyes open. I'll saddle up Checker and go look for Rocky so we don't get any nasty surprises. I can see how far around your property the flooding goes while I'm at it. Find if there's a way out cross-country."

"Here. If you're going riding, you'll need this." She held out a red, white and blue Texas Rangers baseball cap. "To replace the one I lost in the hurricane. I bought it as an early Christmas present for Dad, but I think you'll need it."

"If it's for your dad—"

"It's only August. I'll get to another game." When she smiled like that, he couldn't find it in him to protest.

"Thanks."

She bypassed his outstretched hand and set the cap on his head herself. Nate groaned as she moved in close enough to give his nose a reminder of the maple toaster pastries they'd had for breakfast.

But he stood patiently while she frowned, then turned the bill around to the back. Then she pulled it back to the front. "I don't know which way I like better—the professional man of duty and honor. Or—" she flipped the bill around to the back and tapped her lips as if she was studying some classic work of art "—the boyish, flirty look that shows off those eyes."

Boyish and *flirty* had never been a part of Nate Kellison. Until Jolene.

Even now, he wasn't sure what she saw in his old soul that made her think he could ever be young and carefree. But he felt like trying.

He plucked the cap from her grasp and turned it around, pulling the brim low enough to shade his eyes.

"How about the let's-get-down-to-business-and-get-some-work-done look?"

She stood back and grinned in a way that tickled him down to his toes. "That works, too. You want me to get the horses?"

She'd gotten down to the second step before he grabbed her by the elbow and stopped her. He circled around and stood on the ground in front of her, meeting her at eye level and blocking her path.

"No. One horse. You're staying here to check the other animals while I ride out." He deftly changed the subject before she could argue. "Did you have any luck contacting your father?"

She raised an eyebrow indignantly, telling him she recognized the diversion tactic for what it was. But she answered, anyway. "The ground lines and cell phone are both still out of order. I wish I hadn't left my truck at Lily's so we could try the radio again."

"That truck couldn't have made it over the roads, much less cross-country the way we came yesterday."

"I know. I just feel so isolated. No communication, no running water. And since the generators have run out of juice, no electricity. Just us."

Was the *us* a good thing or a bad thing? Not wanting to dwell on the possible answer, Nate released her. "There's a lot to be said for peace and quiet."

She crossed her arms and squinched up her face in a disbelieving frown.

Oh, right, Nate thought. "Peace" and "quiet" probably weren't in her vocabulary.

"Let's get to work," she said. "I'll try to reach Dad again a little later." Her defensive posture melted in a heart-deep sigh. "I just hope he's okay. I hope everyone in Turning Point is okay."

Reading her concern, feeling her pain like a wound inside himself, Nate reached out and caught that wayward tendril of golden hair that fell across her downturned face. He rolled the silky strand between his sensitized fingertips before brushing it across her soft cheek and tucking it behind her ear. With a nudge of his palm against her jaw, he tilted her face up to his. "He's probably more worried about you than anything. But I'm sure he's fine. You had to get those lucky, hardheaded survival genes from someone. From the sound of things, I gather your mom isn't the hang-tough-when-the-chips-are-down type."

"Yeah, my dad's the tough one. On the outside, at least." She offered him a game smile that was equal parts gratitude and reassurance. "But I had you to help me. Whether or not I thought I needed you, you turned out to be pretty handy to have around."

Nate shrugged and let his hand slide down to cup the side of her neck. "Well, what's left of me, anyway."

Jolene's smile flatlined. "Don't do that."

Snatching his hand away, Nate wondered how he'd overstepped the boundaries of familiarity when they'd held each other for warmth and comfort all through the night. "Sorry."

"Don't put yourself down. Don't pretend that there's something broken or inferior about you. You're not disabled."

"Jolene—"

"I've seen you in action, cowboy." She pricked up like a scrawny hen defending her nest, skin flushed, blue eyes blazing. She poked him harmlessly in a bruise-free spot at the center of the chest, and he wisely retreated a step. "And while I'm sorry that your leg's busted and your shoulder's torn up and you've got a lot to deal with on the inside, that's not what I see when I look at you."

Nate propped his hands on his hips. He'd gotten lectures like this from his sister. But then, Jackie was his sister. She was supposed to jump his case from time to time to get him off his pity pot.

"Okay, Miss Smarty-Pants. Tell me what you think you see. And then I'll get you straight to the ophthalmologist."

Jolene counted the points off on her fingers. "Your eyes. Gorgeous color and they say a lot. Right now I'm ignoring their message, but it's coming through loud and clear."

He narrowed said eyes into a skeptical frown as she hit finger number two.

"Broad shoulders. They have to be with all the responsibility you insist on carrying on them."

Third finger. He wasn't convinced. "Hands. They…well, they…" Her cheeks seared a rosy pink. She inhaled a deep, steadying breath that shamelessly drew his gaze to the rise of her breasts. She swallowed hard. He took note of that movement, too. "I seem to recall mentioning magic of some kind."

Jolene had made the magic, Nate realized. She *was* the magic. He'd just responded to it. Helplessly. Hungrily.

In a flash of vivid memory, Nate pictured all the things his hands had done to her on the couch, all the things he still wanted to do. And later that night, the way he'd simply gotten to massage her neck, to hold her through the trailing edge of the storm. He'd found a comfort, a sense of peace that was every bit as humbling as her body's feverish reactions to the stroke of his hands and mouth.

Things were getting stiff behind the zipper of his jeans again. And despite every common sense rule he tried to apply to his life, his palms itched with the desire to touch her again. To reclaim the feeling of home and heaven that he'd found with Jolene in his arms.

Nate wavered. Jackie's talks never went like this.

Jolene held up the fourth finger. "Your backside."

"My backside?"

"That's right. Your tush." Now she was making light of things again, talking up a streak to press her point. "I took an informal survey among eligible females here on the ranch, and we decided we like the view going as much as we like the one heading toward us."

"*We* decided?"

"Take the compliment, California. And don't put yourself down in front of me again. Now get out of here. I have work to do."

Nate wanted to believe she saw him as this studly guy who could deliver. But it was just the situation talking. The whole Adam and Eve thing. Being the only man and woman for miles probably made him look pretty good for a change. They'd been forced together by disaster and had stuck together to survive, just as Turning Point's very first settlers had.

But someone handsomer, more whole, and a helluva lot more *boyish* would show up once the flood waters receded. Then he'd revert to being Jolene's beat-up partner and unwanted protector. And maybe, just maybe, a friend.

But he wouldn't hope for anything more. He'd be a sucker if he believed half of what she'd just said about him.

But she was right about one thing. The sun would get hot by the afternoon. They'd better get to work.

Nate had always been able to set aside his own needs and fears to get the job done. "When I get back, I won't find you up on the roof trying to patch the leaks and re-place the shingles, will I?"

"I don't know. It depends on how long it takes you to fix things up out here and track down Rocky. I'm going to check the animals first. Then I'll find the ladder."

"Jolene—"

"Just kidding. Well, a little. I want to clean up the liv-ing room and the kitchen. Then I'll tackle the roof."

"No." Man, she was killing him with this kind of teas-ing. At least he prayed she was teasing. Even though the storm had passed, his duties watching over Jolene Kan-non-Angel clearly weren't finished. "Stay off the roof."

"Work fast," she countered, without giving him the promise he needed to hear. "I'll wait as long as I can for you to help me."

"Uh-uh. No ladders, no roof."

She gave him a gentle nudge back toward the barn. "You'd better get started on that pen. I promise, no climbing until you're there to hold the ladder."

"No climbing, period."

"Go. And don't let Rocky catch you unaware."

Maybe he did believe a little of what she'd said. Be-fore she could turn to march back up the steps, Nate snaked his hand behind her neck, tunneled his fingers into the root of her braid and tipped her head back for his kiss.

It was a perfunctory meeting of mouths and spirits. She braced her hands at his waist, curled her fingers through his belt loops. Her lush lips parted beneath his and he staked his claim—for the moment—and informed her in no uncertain terms that he meant business. When he pulled away, he took her moist heat, her breathless sigh, and the sweet, maple taste of her with him.

She couldn't ignore his message now. Or the worry behind it. "No roof."

"Okay."

Okay? She was agreeing with him? Promising?

He withdrew his fingers from the silken snare of her braid. She unhooked her grasp on him and hugged her arms around her belly.

"Okay." He confirmed her answer, not quite believing it.

With one last warning look, he turned away and pulled on his gloves. He'd better work fast to get Rocky's new home repaired and the bull secured inside. As soon as that task was completed, Nate intended to hustle his butt back to the house to help Jolene before she broke her neck or hurt the baby.

As he strode across the yard with an awkward gait, he glanced over his shoulder. He could feel the admiring heat focused on his fanny. Hell. She *was* looking.

Don't pretend that there's something broken or inferior about you. You're not disabled.

If it was possible for a man with a crooked leg and a lot on his conscience to do it, Nate pulled back his shoulders and walked a little taller.

Crazy what that woman could make him feel.

Crazy.

"DO *NOT* FALL IN LOVE with him," Jolene reminded herself, pounding the last nail into the plywood she'd used to cover the shattered front window. "You'll regret it. Don't do it."

She dropped the hammer into Joaquin's old toolbox and wished the clank and rattle of steel on steel would startle the useless notion right out of her head.

It was just a kiss! Her mouth tingled at the memory. Pressing her lips together, she tried to erase the flood of warmth and anticipation she couldn't quite seem to shake. Okay, so there'd been more than one kiss. And he didn't seem to think she'd been a total klutz about the whole man-woman intimacy thing, either.

Jolene brushed her hand against her neck, remembering the gentle touch of his callused fingertips there. Her own fingers drifted down into the vee of her blouse, following the trail he'd taken last night on the couch. The weight of her palm against her breast triggered an instantaneous reaction deep inside her. Jolene snatched her hand away when the sound of her own breathy moan reached her ears.

Okay, so there'd been a whole lot more than kissing going on.

"Boy, am I in trouble."

She hurriedly squatted down to clean up the rest of her mess.

It was that stray puppy syndrome, she rationalized, opening a black garbage bag and dumping the trash inside. Nate was wounded, inside and out. She'd been drawn to the need she perceived in him. He needed her tears, her stern words, her comfort. She could help him see himself through new eyes. She could make him grin, get him to talk. He'd even been touched when she'd wrapped up a sandwich and some fresh fruit and taken him lunch out in the barn when he'd been too busy to come inside to eat.

That's what attracted her to him. He needed her.

People who needed her wouldn't leave.

Her heavy sigh stirred the dust she'd swept into the bag. "Oh, boy."

It had come back to this, had it?

She hadn't been what her mother needed. She hadn't been able to give Joaquin what he needed. Not in time.

Jolene cradled the baby, feeling each loss as fresh as if it had happened yesterday.

"Don't let Mama do this, sweetie."

Closing the trash bag, she pushed herself to her feet. She hadn't been able to sweep aside any of the confounding, wonderful feelings churning inside her now.

She needed Nate, too. That was the kicker.

She needed to work beside him. To butt heads with him. To talk with him late into the night. To be held by him. To lust after him and have him lust after her.

"Oh, damn. Damn, damn." The realization echoed throughout her empty house.

"Shh. You didn't hear that," she whispered to the baby.

She'd already fallen in love with Nate Kellison.

And her feelings didn't have a darn thing to do with stray puppies.

JOLENE GATHERED THE REST of Joaquin's tools and hurried out to the garage, trying to leave the newly discovered emotions behind. She grabbed the kerosene and the grill lighter from a shelf and went out back to start a

bonfire out of all the unusable debris she'd piled from
the house and yard.

The acrid smell of sulphur and chemicals stung her
nose and made her eyes water. After a couple of tries,
the fire ignited. For a long time, the soaked wood merely
smoked, creating a gray, billowing cloud that rose into
the air, blocking the sun and reminding her of the approach of yesterday's storm.

But eventually, the tattered gingham that had once
been her living room curtains flamed up. By the time
the dollhouse that had blown into the yard had mutated
into a charred black skeleton, some of the broken barn
planks were burning. The big limb that had crashed
through her window would catch next.

Jolene stood at a safe distance and watched the bonfire, mesmerized by the dancing blaze, entranced by
the hiss and pop of drying wood and bubbling sap and
inevitable ignition. She was lulled into a groggy, hyp-
notic state by the growing heat that toasted her face and
body but couldn't purge her heart of its foolish longings.

Off in the distance a coyote howled.

Suddenly alert, Jolene opened her eyes.

Not so distant.

Her pulse and attention leaped back into real time
and she spun around, trying to pinpoint the direction of
the howl.

Nate had returned from his morning ride with Rocky
in tow and the news that beyond about a mile radius in
any direction, they were surrounded by flood water.
The one exception was the eastern drop-off into Livesay
Canyon, named for the wagon train master responsible
for bringing Turning Point's earliest residents together.

And Nate had reported hearing water running off into the creek at the bottom of the canyon. Mother Nature had imprisoned them for the time being.

Sliding one hand down to protect her belly, Jolene backed toward the house, keeping her eyes peeled for any signs of movement. "We're not the only ones trapped by the flood."

The fire had probably caught the coyote's attention and made him nervous. But it should also help keep him at bay, until the waters receded and he could find his way out to open territory.

She just hoped the dogs didn't get a hankering to chase the wild animal. Speaking of Broody and Shasta…"I'd better go chain them up."

After putting away the lighter and fuel, she rinsed her hands in a bucket of water and headed across the yard. As she walked, she gazed from side to side, vaguely wondering what other unfriendly critters had gotten trapped in their little Texas Eden by the storm and floods.

"I know you qualify." Jolene pointed an accusatory finger at Rocky in his makeshift pen. Her teasing was beneath him, judging by the way he continued scratching his mud-caked hide against one of the rails Nate had rigged between the metal posts that were still firmly anchored in the ground.

Jolene wasn't worried that the coyote would be a threat to Rocky. The bull would make quick work of any creature that size who foolishly wandered into his pen. The barn cats were another matter, however. And Shasta, feisty and tough as he tried to be, would make a tasty-size morsel for a coyote hungry enough to venture up to the house and barn. Broody, the lab, wasn't a fighter, but he'd be big enough to give any intruder a run for the money.

But whether they wound up predator or prey, Jolene didn't want any of her little darlings to get hurt. Pursing her lips together, she gave a whistle. "Broody! Here, boy. Shasta!"

Their answering barks told her they were in the barn. The fact that they didn't come running to her call told her that Nate was there, too. The dogs had been following him around all day, instantly switching loyalties to their new guest after a few commands in Nate's no-nonsense voice and some rough and tumble games of fetch and wrestle.

Jolene sighed at the stab of loneliness that caught her by surprise.

Even the dogs had left her.

"Good grief, girl, get a grip." She chastised herself at the fanciful notion, wishing her heart would take heed of her brain's warning. She had to find a way to turn off those emotions and simply survive her and Nate's remaining time together.

He was probably still up on the barn roof, patching the holes with sheets of plywood and temporarily waterproofing them with a tarp. Thankfully, her insurance and savings were intact. It was going to cost a small fortune to make the more permanent repairs that the house and ranch needed after Hurricane Damon had had his way. In the meantime, Nate had worked his very nice butt off making things livable again.

No, no, no, she cautioned herself. She couldn't start thinking about Nate and the Double J and the future and staying.

"Find the dogs, Jolene." She reminded herself she

was looking for four-legged males, not the two-legged kind. "You're here to find the dogs."

Sliding through the opening between the barn doors, Jolene stepped inside and paused a moment to let her eyes adjust to the cool, shady interior. The pungent smells of hay and horses teased her nose and soothed her senses. She breathed in deeply, finding strength and serenity in the familiar scents.

Okay, she could do this. Jolene smiled, feeling a little less morose, a little more in control.

She whistled again. "Broody. Shasta."

The two dogs came running from opposite corners of the barn. Shasta, the scrappy little fuzz mop with intelligent eyes and a stiff-legged gait, reached Jolene first. Broody, a big, tan pony of a dog loped behind him, his tongue lolling out the side of his mouth.

"There you are." Jolene squatted down and petted each one thoroughly, earning adoring snuggles and happy woofs as she traded tummy rubs and ear scratches for renewed loyalty and affection. "Have you boys been busy? Come with Mama."

Broody and Shasta trotted faithfully behind her as she hooked them up to the long leads that would secure them to the barn and give them access to food, water and a place to nap. They both agreed to a dog biscuit as a fair trade-off for limiting their running space.

Once the dogs were happily distracted, Jolene went in search of Nate. The footsteps and hammering on the roof two stories above her let her know exactly where she'd find him.

Dust and chips of wood and hay filtered down through the cracks in the roof and the loft overhead. She looked up to see fingers of sunlight shining in through a chink of roof. "Hmm. Mother Nature made me a skylight."

Not that a hole in the roof over the section of the loft where she stored bales of hay was a practical thing. But there was something oddly romantic about a sun-warmed bed of hay in the secluded corner of the barn. It was like a small gift from Mother Nature after wreaking so much havoc in every other corner of the Double J.

A flash of shadow disrupted the celestial beauty of the light. That was Nate moving overhead. He'd been working all day without a proper break. Shouldering more responsibility than any one man should have to.

Jolene picked up the thermos of water and untouched apple left over from Nate's lunch and crossed to the wooden ladder leading up to the loft. On impulse, she pulled a blanket from a tack hook and carried it with her.

At the base of the ladder, she debated logistics for all of about five seconds, then stuffed the apple down the front of her blouse and buttoned it in. She looped the blanket around her neck, clenched the thermos firmly in her left hand and climbed.

Ten rungs later, Jolene stepped off onto the loft platform. "Nate?" She set the thermos on a nearby bale and spread the blanket out over the bed of loose hay covering the floor of the loft. Dozens of dust motes shimmered in the rays of sunlight above the spot, creating an ethereal atmosphere around her. "Nate?" she repeated, squinting up into the square of sunlight above her. "You should come see this. It's beautiful. Nate?"

Was that a curse?

"Jolene?" Quick, uneven footsteps pounded overhead, sending a considerably less magical cloud of dust down over her head. She had to blink and turn away. She jumped back a step, midsneeze, as a red metal toolbox dropped through the opening and crashed to the loft floor, stirring up more dust and shaking the planks beneath her feet. "Jolene Kannon-Angel, I swear to God…"

A pair of brown work boots, attached to long, muscular legs, dropped through the hole next. Then, a naked back. A few black and blue spots marred the smooth ripple of muscles, but the sheen of healthy perspiration actually enhanced the impression of masculine strength. Broad shoulders, sturdy triceps and a royal blue cap followed as Nate lowered himself through the roof.

Jolene's lips parted involuntarily. Her father's old jeans cupped Nate's backside, yet left an oddly erotic strip of trim, white cotton brief showing at the waistband. She clenched her thighs together, caught off guard by a sudden gush of dampness and heat.

"I just wanted…" She began, but a grunt of pain drew her attention to the stark white bandage at the top of his tanned shoulder. "Does it hurt?" Duh. "Sorry." She swallowed the apology on a nervous laugh.

But he wasn't smiling when he turned around.

His glance at the ladder told her exactly where this discussion was headed. "I swear, woman. You promised—"

"I promised I wouldn't climb up the ladder to the roof of the house."

"You—" He sputtered, snapping his mouth shut to rethink his argument. "You—" He peeled off his cap, smoothed his palm across his dark hair, then jerked the cap back into place. Jolene curled her toes inside her boots and held her ground when he advanced a step, his gaze centered squarely on the swell of her belly. "What about the baby?"

"He climbed up with me just fine." She found her own nerves calming in the face of his protective anger. "We appreciate your concern, but we are both fine. You're the one who needs to take a break. It's okay if you abdicate responsibility for a few minutes and relax." She pointed to the opening above his head. "The sunlight streaming in makes this a beautiful place to rest."

Instead of glancing up, Nate dropped his gaze to the red plaid blanket beneath his feet. He took note of the steel thermos and the bales of hay surrounding the two of them. His chest heaved in a weary sigh that emphasized the flat bronze nipples peeking out through a T-shaped mat of curly dark hair. Before she could close her eyes, Jolene had followed the narrowing trail of hair until it disappeared into the waistband behind the snap of his jeans.

Whoa.

Nate had fallen as silent as she had.

The air seemed close. Her pulse hammered in her ears.

Suddenly, the sunny spot didn't feel like a warm, magical place of rest, but something decidedly hotter. Secluded. Intimate. She didn't know what to do about it, but she understood the sultry invitation hanging in the air between them.

Nate understood, too.

"Jolene." His voice was a throaty rumble that shivered along her spine. "I don't think—"

In a burst of nervous energy, Jolene pulled the apple out of her blouse and held it out to him in her open palm. "I thought you might be hungry."

CHAPTER TEN

JOLENE HELD OUT the shiny red apple like Eve offering temptation itself.

Nate couldn't think straight. He couldn't get past the hungry perusal of her eyes, the erratic rhythm of her breathing—or his own fiercely male reaction to her sweetly parted lips and not-so-innocent invitation.

His throat felt tight, his mouth dry. His stomach was a knot of tension and his groin ached with the need to possess her, seduce her, teach her how to complete what her soft voice and eager hands and hungry eyes had started last night.

"I've never done this before," she blurted out, snatching the apple back to her chest and blushing a bright, rosy pink.

Her announcement put the brakes on his out-of-control hormones and startled a bit of rational thinking into his head. He didn't have to ask what *this* meant. She'd been thinking hot, steamy sex just like he had. But *this* didn't make sense.

He looked down at her belly. "You're pregnant."

She nodded. Then she clutched both hands around the apple and crinkled her face in an apologetic frown. "In vitro fertilization. Joaquin and I never had sex. *I've* never had sex. I've done some heavy petting, but not with my husband. And not very often. I don't date much. Well, even before I was married, I didn't. Once you get a reputation in a small town as a good girl or best friend, guys don't…"

She paused for a breath. "Joaquin was already so sick and he said he wouldn't demand anything. We were good buddies since high school so I knew we would get along as a couple. And he needed a bone marrow transplant, so we went to the justice of the peace and then we went to Houston and…"

Now she was gesturing with the apple. "His sperm and my…well, you probably know how that's done. But he died before… We waited too long. Now I'm having his baby. Make no mistake, I love this little guy. I want him more than anything. But I never…"

Nate listened until she ran out of gas, then translated her rambling into a message he could understand.

"You're a pregnant virgin?"

She rolled her eyes and waved her hands in the air. "Woo-hoo. Freaky me. Call the Guinness Book of World Records."

"Stop it." Nate closed the distance between them. He gently seized her flailing hands and pried the apple from her grasp. "You and your husband never…?"

"Nope." She pulled her hands free and hugged herself. "And I'm probably not going to right now, am I?"

Stunned was Nate's first reaction.

He passed by a moment of disbelief.

But as he replayed everything he knew about this woman—her eagerness to help anyone in need, her willingness to set aside what was best for herself to help that person, her endearing lack of experience and enthusiastic desire to learn each time they'd gotten close—he realized she was telling the truth.

Acceptance followed.

Then he savored the greedier emotions building inside him. The absolution from guilt. A bereaved friend wasn't the same thing as a bereaved widow. The thrill of discovery. She could be his in a way no other woman ever had been. The blossoming of hope. Jolene Kannon-Angel and her baby were two miracles who had careened into his world and given him a purpose. They breathed fresh energy into the doldrums of his life. He felt younger. Whole.

Home.

Despite her downturned face and embarrassed cheeks, Jolene kept glancing up to read his reaction. Hadn't she listened to his secrets last night? Tended his wounds? Cried for his pain? Nurtured his battered pride?

"For God's sake, say something," she begged.

He owed her one.

He owed *them* one.

Nate didn't intend to disappoint.

He rubbed the apple against his thigh, then flipped it around in his hand until he found a firm spot. Sinking his teeth through the sleek skin and juicy flesh, he took a greedy bite. He crunched the tart, ripe fruit between his teeth and wiped the succulent juice from his lips with the back of his hand.

Jolene's eyes followed every move. The rhythm of her breathing changed. Her lower lip trembled, and everything potent and masculine inside him quaked in response.

Nate swallowed.

"I am hungry." His voice sounded like the growly promise of thunder to his ears.

Jolene tipped up her chin in anticipation. *Inexperienced,* he reminded himself.

But great instincts.

Nate tossed the apple aside. He thrust his fingers into the hair at her nape and pulled her mouth up to his.

She came up on her toes and braced her hands at his waist as he crushed her lips beneath his. He swept his tongue inside her mouth and caressed soft, wet skin and hard, straight teeth. Her tongue darted out to catch his and play tag.

Her palms were cool against his sun-warmed skin. She dragged them along his flanks, slid them together against his stomach, pushed them higher over the swell of his pecs. Nate sucked in his breath at the insistent press of the heels of her palms against his nipples.

She snatched her hands away with a gasp of disappointment. "I'm sorry. Did I hurt—?"

Nate dragged her hands right back to the sensitive nubs and rubbed her against him. "That feels amazing," he breathed against her temple, catching that silky strand of hair with his nose. "You touch me, angel," he instructed, dropping his head to reclaim her mouth, "however you want."

"Like this?" A quick student, Jolene took over the sensuous massage, rolling the buds between her fingers and zapping lightning bolts of desire straight to his groin. She learned the trick of alternating each stimulating stroke with a gentler caress so that the intensity of that lightning increased with each touch.

"Oh, yeah." He slid his hands down either side of her

neck and let his fingers stray beneath the collar of her shirt to trace the delicate arch of her shoulder. "Just like that."

Her breasts drifted closer to the hard wall of his chest. Through the thin layers of her blouse and bra, the beaded tips teased his skin, sending tiny shocks jolting along every nerve ending.

He tipped her head farther back to suckle the wide, lush bounty of her lower lip. He stroked his thumbs along the smooth column of her throat and felt the vibration of her delight humming beneath the skin. "You're so responsive, angel," he praised her. "You make me feel more of a man than I really am."

She moaned against his mouth, then pulled her lips away with a noisy smack. Her eyes were hazy, turbulent with gathering clouds of passion. "We talked about that," she scolded. She slid her hands beneath his arms, skidded them along his spine, then reached down and grabbed two deliberate handfuls of his tush. Nate jerked, helplessly thrusting his hip against hers. "You *feel* perfect to me."

Catching up with the student, Nate took the same liberties with Jolene. He slid his hands down her long back, over the flare of her hips, and palmed the sweet, ripe curves of that beautiful butt.

"You're not so bad yourself," he said. Jolene gasped as he squeezed and lifted her up against his swollen heat. "I want you, angel." He whispered the husky plea against her ear and kissed her there, then rubbed himself shamelessly against her. Her eyes widened in unexpected bliss and her head fell back. Nate lowered her lips to kiss her throat, tonguing the hot, rapid beat of her pulse. "I want you now."

She was nodding, clutching at him, twisting her hips. "Yes," she whispered, raking her fingers into his hair, shoving aside his ball cap and guiding his mouth back to hers. "Yes, Nate. Yes."

Suddenly they were a flurry of hands and kisses, touching this, unbuttoning that. Nate sank to his knees in the middle of the blanket and pulled Jolene down with him, kissing her all the way.

She threw her arms around his neck and her body slid down the length of his. Every cell in him sprang to attention, and he absorbed every maddening detail about her. The soft give of her firm breasts. The pebbly-hard nubs at the tip of each peak. The thrust of her small belly. The rosy color of her lips and the flush of passion on her cheeks.

The swelling in his knee had lessened, but the damn ache would always be with him. After a few charged moments—just long enough to undo her hair and let it fall around his face and shoulders—he surrendered to the demands of his body and laid her on the floor. With barely a grunt of pain, he came down beside her. He threw his bum leg over both of hers and spread himself wider, nudging her hips into the vee of his legs.

With reverent attention to every soft, beautiful inch of skin, he slowly peeled off her blouse. He slipped one bra strap off her shoulder, and then the other. But when he tucked his fingers into the lacy cups and started to pull, panic replaced the passion in her eyes and her hands shot up to cover herself.

"Don't." It was a husky whisper of raw self-awareness. But she kept her gaze locked on his. "Maybe you should try somewhere else. Do something different. Even with the baby, they're not—"

"Shh." Nate pressed his finger against her lips to stop the protest. "They're perfect. Exactly the size and shape I've been looking for," he teased.

"Nate."

Keeping her tucked firmly in the scissor-hold of his legs, he leaned back and let the sunlight from above shine down on her. With the gentlest touch his eager fingers could manage, he stripped the bra off her, then feasted his eyes on her beautiful body, from the puckered, rosy tips of each breast to the fertile swell of her belly.

The sun dappled her naked skin, giving her a golden glow. He touched his finger to one bright spot and felt her shiver. When she'd quieted, he touched another. The tip of her chin, the indentation at the base of her throat, the subtle valley between her breasts.

"Nate." His name on that hopeful, husky plea thickened his blood and sent it pulsing through him.

She liked a good argument. Nate summoned a grin and used her own words against her. "The males on this ranch took an informal survey. And we decided you're the sexiest thing in the entire state of Texas."

"We?"

"Me." He rocked his hips over hers, but fought to hold himself back. "*I* think you're sexy. The other guys have to find their own woman."

"Don't encourage Rocky—"

"Forget the bull." In more ways than one. He was burning with the need to do this. Now. "This is you and me and the Texas sun. Nobody else."

He palmed her breast. She trembled. "Everything about you…" He kissed the other breast. Her knees jerked up; her fingers dug into his shoulder and chest. "Is perfect."

"Nate—"

He stopped her protest with a kiss. He wasn't going to hear any arguments about not being pretty enough. He just couldn't see it. "You sure you want a beat-up old warhorse like me to be the one?"

She framed his face between her hands. "I've never wanted anyone else. Not like this."

Jolene pulled him in for a tender kiss that quickly spun out of control. Nate kicked off his boots and freed himself from his jeans. When she wrapped a curious hand around his aching shaft, he nearly came unglued. "Easy, angel."

"Hurry, Nate."

He got rid of her jeans and panties and slipped his fingers inside her tight, weeping channel. She was primed to explode and so was he. He bent her knees up and slipped between them, propping himself up on his elbows to protect the child inside her.

"This might hurt some," he cautioned, nudging her slick heat.

She wrapped her arms around him and pulled him down, demanding a kiss. He eased himself in partway, retreated.

"More." She nibbled the jut of his chin, thrust her hips beneath his. "More."

He pushed in again, farther. Retreated.

"Nate!"

He grinned at her sharp, breathy request.

Swirling torrents of white-hot need clashed with the soul-healing power of her acceptance—her desire— for him.

He plunged in a third time and found retreat was no

longer an option. He buried himself to the hilt, meeting every thrust of her hips, loving every greedy demand of her hands and mouth.

Again and again he took what she offered and gave back everything in return until the storm building between them struck with full force. Jolene arched her neck and cried out, the tremors inside her cascading all around him. Nate ground his hips, threw back his head and emptied himself inside her.

When he could think once more, Nate rolled onto his back and gathered Jolene in his arms to rest on top of him. Her legs tangled with his. She fingered the bandage on his shoulder and sucked in deep, calming breaths. He secured her against him with one hand on her bottom and the other at her neck beneath the tangled, silky fall of her hair. A gentle breeze through the roof cooled their sticky skin.

"I feel so good. I…I liked it. A lot." She groaned and buried her face in his chest. He could feel the heat rising in her cheeks. "Oh, God, that sounded so naive."

Nate tipped her chin up and kissed her forehead. He looked deep into those blue eyes, feeling humbled by her honesty. "It sounded like a mighty nice compliment. And if it means anything to you, I liked it, too. A lot."

Her answering smile forgave sins and sparked dreams. But he wasn't ready to leave the moment and face either one right now. So he kissed her once more and tucked her up tight against him.

Nate willingly held her until she grew heavy and he knew she'd drifted off to sleep. The baby stirred between them and Nate adjusted their positions to give the little guy room to maneuver.

But he couldn't quite let go of her. Not yet. He knew he was holding something precious in his arms, something he'd only recently discovered. Something he wasn't ready to lose.

Crazy Texas woman. Losing her virginity in a barn loft after a hurricane had decimated her home and left her stranded with no amenities whatsoever.

Giving that gift to him.

Crazy.

He pulled the ends of the blanket loosely over their bodies, kissed her closed eyelids and cuddled her close beneath the last rays of sunshine streaming in through the roof.

Crazy wonderful.

JOLENE PICKED UP the dirty paper plates and blew out the candles on the kitchen table, temporarily plunging the room into darkness and erasing the lingering image of the awkward dinner she'd shared with Nate. Their conversation had been stilted and polite, on topics ranging from food and supply lists to seasonal weather expectations.

Neither of them had said much about what had happened in the barn, beyond his report that she'd dozed for about twenty minutes and that he'd have to get back on the roof in the morning since he'd run out of daylight to complete the job. As eagerly as they'd stripped off their clothes and explored each other's bodies, they'd made a point of turning their backs to each other and hurriedly dressing.

Jolene couldn't tell if that was the practical side of Nate—after all, he'd insisted on carting everything back

down the ladder for her, then climbing down a few rungs
ahead of her in case she lost her grip or missed her footing. Or whether the reality of what he'd just done—and
who he'd done it with—had set in along with regret.

The dinner itself had been a delicious concoction of
stew from one of his Grandpa Nate's secret recipes.
Nate had tossed in just about every type of meat and
vegetable they had on hand so that nothing would go to
waste now that the contents of her freezer had thawed.
Jolene's plate was embarrassingly clean, even after two
helpings and a serving of "creme brulee" made from a
pudding cup, brown sugar and the lighter for the grill—
Nate's creation. Her ravenous appetite was the result of
pregnancy and hard work—and the emotional and physical drain of having sex.

Great sex.

Change-her-life-in-one-orgasmic-rush-and-cuddle-
like-she-was-in-love-afterward sex.

"Oh, Lordy."

Jolene flipped on the switch of a battery-powered
lantern, knowing that standing around in the dark and
reliving every moment before, during and after the event
wasn't going to improve her situation any.

The lantern flooded the kitchen with a cool, yellow-
ish light that hinted at secrets and shadows and un-
known hazards beyond the edges of its illumination. It
was nothing like the warm, cocooning rays of sunshine
that had warmed her body and wrapped her in a hopeful spell up in the loft that afternoon with Nate.

She'd made love to a man.

He'd made love to her.

She'd lost her freaky status as Turning Point's first

and only pregnant virgin. She'd lost a few of those self-conscious doubts about her own sexuality.

She'd lost her heart. Sealed the deal completely. Set herself up to be hurt in ways that a mother's abandonment and a good friend's death couldn't touch. Jolene had been too young to fully comprehend her mother's choice, and she hadn't had the skills or the miracle up her sleeve to save Joaquin's life.

But she could have kept her feelings for Nate in check. They could have stayed friends and coexisted at a less intimate level if she'd been paying closer attention. But, no, like everything else, she'd jumped in with both feet and no life jacket and fallen in love with the guy. She'd listened to her heart and trusted her gut and completely ignored common sense and the inevitable pain headed her way.

She'd known him for thirty-six hours. Thirty-six! And they'd barely gotten along for the first twelve. There were men in Turning Point she'd known all of her twenty-eight years whom she'd never even considered dating. And now she'd not only slept with this stranger, she'd given him her heart.

"Idiot."

Jolene wrapped up the leftover stew and placed it in an ice chest. She'd insisted on cleaning up, since Nate had cooked. It was only fair. Besides, if he wasn't in the mood to say much, she wasn't in the mood for listening to silence.

Now he was washing up in the bathroom, sponging himself off with the basin of water they'd set aside for bathing. He was probably in there naked. Naked and gorgeous from the front or the back and counting the dings and bruises on his body that she was directly or indirectly responsible for. Washing her scent off his body and planning the next home-repair project that would keep him busy and away from her dangerous, overenthusiastic, unwanted attentions.

Sex was one thing.

Commitment was something else.

Nate Kellison lived in California. He had family he loved there. He had an important job.

She was a small-town Texas girl with a baby on the way. She had a legacy to rebuild and maintain for her son. She had a single father who needed her. This was where she had to stay.

California. Texas.

Nate. Jolene.

Big trouble.

He was going to leave her.

Gripping the edge of the table, Jolene held on as fearful anticipation buffeted through her. She hugged her baby and blinked back the sting of tears. "Oh, Dad. I wish I could talk to you right now."

She needed Mitch Kannon's patient ear and fatherly hug and hopeful reminder that not everyone she loved left her.

But once the flood waters receded, once the state of emergency had been terminated, Nate would have no reason to stay. A few long talks and some amazing sex couldn't erase all the arguments, or the injuries, or the impulsive mistakes, or the lack of experience with men that made her more of a project than a helpmate.

Wait a minute.

"Dad?" A new thought popped into Jolene's head,

momentarily putting the brakes on the downward spiral of her emotions. Could Nate think that he'd broken his promise to her father? That he'd stepped beyond the boundaries of *taking care* of her?

Was it possible that Nate's polite withdrawal had more to do with the value of his word than with her?

He could be plain old tired.

He might feel guilty.

Things might be moving way too quickly for a thoughtful guy like Nate.

Or…she could be the problem.

Suffused with renewed energy, Jolene picked up the lantern and patted her tummy. "Let's go find out."

Hurrying through the familiar rooms in her bare feet, Jolene entered the master bedroom and crossed straight to the bathroom door. She had her fist raised to knock when she heard him moving around inside, knocking something over, muttering beneath his breath.

Maybe she'd better let him finish his business before she demanded answers. She pulled her hand back to her side and turned off the lantern. Patience really wasn't her strong suit, but for this, she could wait.

Padding back across the carpet, she climbed up onto the blue and white quilt that covered her four-poster bed, leaned against one of the polished oak posts and planned what she wanted to say.

Her eyes had adjusted to the moonlit darkness by the time the bathroom door opened.

She popped up off the bed the instant Nate appeared.

"Can we talk about what happened in the barn?"

"Talk?" He froze in the doorway.

She stood close enough to see that he'd shaved. The

two-day growth of beard was gone, along with a couple of nicks of skin. Apparently, he'd braved the cold water, disposable shaver route. But she didn't ask if he'd found the shaving cream stored beneath the sink or borrowed some lotion to smooth the burn.

She looked straight into those whiskey-brown eyes. "Even if I don't like your answers, I need to hear them."

"I'm not dressed."

Jolene followed his gaze as he glanced down at the white towel wrapped around his hips and held together with his fist.

She swallowed hard, feeling light-headed from a rush of heat. Wow, there was a lot of man showing there. And it all seemed to be leanly sculpted around one very fit body.

She took in the mean red cut on his shoulder and the neat white stitching that held it together. She noted the flat stomach and the indented belly button two or more inches above the edge of that terry cloth. And though his most vulnerable parts were covered, the towel slit apart and revealed a long, muscular thigh, misshapen knee and length of leg covered in a patchwork of shiny scars that caught and reflected the moonlight.

Jolene felt her heart clutch at the marks of so much suffering, even as it quickened at the sight of all that muscle and skin. "I didn't see these this afternoon." She reached out to touch one wound, to offer comfort. "Oh, Nate. I'm so sorry."

"Whoa." He put out his hand to ward hers off and jumped back a step. "Can't we put this off for a little while? You know, get a good night's sleep and talk in the morning?"

What? Jolene shifted her gaze back to the firm warning in his eyes. He didn't want her to touch him. Fine. She could live with that.

No, she couldn't.

She shook her head, clearing her thoughts and reminding herself of the reason she was here in the first place. "I need to do this now. There are a couple of things that are making me crazy." Like the fact he was standing in front of her nearly naked, but she wasn't allowed to touch. She shrugged, apologizing for her lousy timing. "Besides, you can't get dressed. I rinsed out your clothes and hung them up to dry. I'm sure they're still damp."

He glanced up at the ceiling and inhaled a deep breath before nailing her with a conversation-closed look. "Jolene, a man likes to have his pants on when he's having a serious discussion."

"So you do think that what happened between us is serious?"

Nate plopped his hand on her shoulder and scooted her out of the way before crossing to the foot of the bed, where he had room to turn around. "Of course, I do. I'm not a guy who sleeps with that many woman."

She whirled around to face him. "So you were just lonely for a woman to sleep with?"

"Don't put words in my mouth."

"Then explain it to me."

"Explain why I made love to you?"

Made love. At least that sounded as if it hadn't been a completely awful or embarrassing experience for him.

Jolene moved closer and hugged her arm around the bedpost. He didn't retreat. Another good sign? Or was he getting angry? "You haven't said much of anything about it."

"I'm not a guy who talks about—"

"I know I came on pretty strong. And then maybe I didn't follow through and make it good enough for you."

"That's not—"

"We haven't known each other for very long. But like you said, I feel I know you better than some people I've known my whole life."

"I know," he agreed. "I feel that, too. But—"

"I thought maybe it had something to do with promising Dad to take care of me. But I'm twenty-eight years old. A grown woman. I'm responsible for my own choices. I can take care of myself."

"What are you say—?"

"Do you regret having sex?"

"It wasn't just sex. Jolene, you're not the kind of a woman that a man—"

"If it isn't me, is there some other reason why you don't want to talk about what happened between—"

"If you want me to talk, let me talk."

His voice was sharp, his expression sharper.

Their coyote friend howled in the silence that followed.

Jolene gnawed on her lip for one nervous moment, then quietly answered. "Okay."

Nate opened his mouth to speak, then hesitated, as if waiting to be interrupted again. Jolene dutifully kept her mouth shut.

"First…" He held up one finger, then seemed to decide it might be wiser to keep both hands on the towel. "I do not regret what happened in the loft. It might not have been the smartest move I've ever made—and yeah,

I've been thinking a lot about being your first and whether or not that was the smartest move *you* could have made. But I wanted to be with you."

"I wanted to be with you, too." Her soft whisper seemed to soothe his patience.

"Second. You were temptation itself, standing there with that shiny red apple and big blue eyes. I'd been working my butt off all day, trying to get you out of my system. After all that talk about liking my ass and being a whole man, I knew I had to keep my distance or I'd do something stupid. But there you were. I wanted you and I couldn't resist." He came a step closer, risked his grip on the towel, and raised one finger to brush the hair off her forehead. "I still can't resist."

"Do you think you'd ever…want to do it again?" She caught his hand when he would have pulled away. "With me?"

Turning his hand, he laced their fingers together and stroked his thumb along the back of her knuckles. "Is that another invitation?"

Jolene pressed her lips together and tried to focus on his eyes instead of the top of that towel and the slight protrusion she could see tenting beneath it. "Would you say yes?"

He raked his gaze over her, staring long enough to make her nipples bead up into tight knots and thrust against the T-shirt she wore. "I'm trying to do the right thing here, angel. It's too soon for you. Even with the procedures you must have had to create that baby, after your first time, things are probably a little tender. We should wait."

"Is that your medical opinion? Or a polite way of putting me off?"

Instead of answering, he dropped his hand to her belly and splayed his fingers there. "How's the baby? I don't want to hurt him, either."

She pressed her hand over his, guiding him to little Joaquin's responsive flutters. "We're both fine."

Nate's fingers trembled with a gentle convulsion against her. He closed his eyes, but Jolene had already seen his pain. "He's so tiny. Helpless. I want him to be strong. Grow tall. Learn how to ride a horse and play some baseball. If something happened to him, I couldn't ..."

A glimmer of understanding pushed aside her own quest for answers. He was holding something back because she was pregnant.

And that terrified him as much as it fascinated him.

Loosing her hold on him and the bed, Jolene reached up to frame his face between her hands. His skin was smooth to the touch now, though the muscles beneath were clenched tight. "Tell me about the baby, Nate."

She didn't have to explain which baby she was talking about. Clearly there was a little one somewhere in the world who haunted him. Moonlight sparkled in the tears he blinked away.

"I lost a little girl," he announced starkly, snatching his hand away from her womb.

"Lost?"

He tapped his hands against her shoulders, then rubbed them up and down her arms, as if he wasn't sure whether to latch on or move away. At last he took her wrists and pulled her hands from his face. "I couldn't save her. There was hardly a mark on her. But she'd been thrown so far from the car. There was too much head and neck trauma. She wasn't breathing. I couldn't get her to breathe."

A tear fell from the corner of his eye and steamed across his angry expression. "We worked that wreck for hours. If we'd gotten the call sooner… If she'd cried out… If we'd known we had to look for her…"

"I'm so sorry." Answering tears burned in Jolene's eyes. "But, Nate, the nature of your job as a paramedic… Sometimes…" She held back her own sorrow, vowing to be strong for him. "Sometimes, there's one you can't save."

He released her on a bitter sigh and paced the room. "This one got to me. I didn't even know she was there. She was still in her car seat, just over the edge of the ditch, out of sight. We were working on her mom. She just quietly died by the side of the road. All alone. I was too late to resuscitate her." He shook his bowed head. "I was too damn late."

Jolene crossed the room behind him. "You can't blame yourself for her death. It was an accident."

"I can't get her face out of my mind—even when I close my eyes, it's always there."

She laid her hand against his back. He flinched, but she used the motion to slip in front of him and silently demand that he look her in the eye and see her faith in him.

"You saved my dad and my home by coming here in the first place. You saved Lily and Amber Browning. You saved Deacon Tate and Cindy and Wes. You nearly got yourself killed saving that stupid bull. Those are memories you should think about, too." She brushed her fingers along the cut side of his jaw. "You saved me and my baby. More than once. Count the miracles, Nate."

"I can't." He grabbed her hand and turned to press a kiss into her palm. Then, with a tug, he gathered her up in his arms and crushed her to his chest. "It's the one who gets away that eats you up inside."

He pulled her ponytail loose and sifted her hair through his fingers. He smelled of clean soap and honest emotion as he rubbed his cheek against hers. With nothing but the towel to cover himself, his arousal bobbed against her belly, thrilling her with his desire, frightening her with the depth of his need. Jolene hugged him tight around the waist and offered whatever she could give.

He dipped his mouth and nuzzled the juncture of her neck and shoulder, melting her bones into putty. His hands slid underneath her shirt, roughly scorching her skin. "It's that one failure that makes me think that the next time, when it counts the most, I won't be able to get the job done. I won't be able to save you."

Jolene frowned. "Save *me?*" *When it counts the most?* Was it wrong to feel a little frisson of hope? Did she count to him? "Nate. I don't need saving."

She tried to push some space between them so she could read his expression. But he'd picked her up and was stumbling backward. She held on so she wouldn't trip him and fall. She'd done enough damage to him already.

"Don't you?" He sank onto the edge of the bed as if the grave responsibility he carried with him was suddenly too much to bear. He fell back across the bed, bringing her down with him. "You're so busy taking care of everybody else—including me—that you don't take care of yourself. You came in here wanting to talk about making love for the first time. And now we're dealing with my crap."

His hands slid beneath the hem of her shirt and he

asked, "Was it good for me? Yes." He worked the shirt up over her head and tossed it aside. "Were you any good? Incredible." Her bra disappeared next and his hungry mouth teased her heated flesh. "Did it change anything between us? Probably. It made me believe this was the way things could be between us. That this was real."

Soon there was nothing but the towel between them. A moment later, not even that. Jolene opened herself to his desperate need. She opened her heart and gave him everything.

"I want *us,* Nate. It doesn't make any sense, but I want there to be an us."

He didn't answer her with words, but his body told her how much he needed her. How much he wanted to be with her. She didn't question herself or him or the moment.

Nate cried out his release deep inside her. Carried her to her own climax. Whispered thanks and praises against her ear as they panted for breath afterward. He pulled her with him under the covers and held her and the baby within the sure grasp of his hands.

Jolene fell asleep knowing that, for tonight at least, she'd been everything he needed.

She'd been enough.

CHAPTER ELEVEN

HE WAS LEAVING.

The sun was shining, the sky was blue, the floods were receding. And he was leaving.

Give her a hurricane any day.

Jolene rubbed her stomach to squelch a nervous sense of dread as she watched Nate saddle up Checker and tie the food and supplies she'd packed for him behind the big bay's saddle.

Technically this wasn't the dramatic wave from the shiny BMW when April Kannon had flipped her blond hair and told her stoic husband and weeping little girl that she just couldn't do this anymore. Sorry.

Nor was it the heart-wrenching quiet of holding Joaquin's cold fingers after his breathing machine had been disconnected and the doctor called his time of death.

Nate was working again. He intended to ride out to check how far the creeks and sloughs had receded to the south to see if he could get through to the Brownings' Rock-a-Bye ranch and make contact with her father and the rest of the outside world.

But it still felt like leaving.

Jolene tried to put on a game face and pretend that surviving forty-eight hours through heaven and hell with this man hadn't changed her life. They knew each other's secrets, their fears, their needs. She knew how much he liked to have his face touched and nuzzled; he knew she had a thing for his butt. She knew he was a talented cook and he knew that her appetite—at least for the next four months or so—was a bottomless pit.

He knew she could be a pretty good listener, despite the way her mouth ran on at times.

And she knew that she loved him.

"Why can't I go with you?" she asked for the umpteenth time since he'd announced his plan over their breakfast of grilled toaster pastries and bacon.

His shoulders rose and fell beneath the snug white T-shirt he wore. When he turned to face her, his voice was patient, his expression kind. "We talked about this. We don't know what conditions are like out there. I'm not thrilled with the idea of you being on a horse over good terrain. What's out there now is anything but good. If we hit a mudslide or washout, or the river's still impassable—or we find another one of Rocky's kinsmen from another ranch running loose—it wouldn't be safe."

"If it gets too tough, I could turn around and come back."

He shook his head. "Then you'd be riding alone, and that would make me crazy, too. I need you and the baby to be safe so that I can concentrate on my bearings and find a way out of here. The milk's gone, the well's flooded and we're running out of fresh water. We've still got no phone line or electricity. We need help, Jolene. I'm going to go find it. We can't live like this forever."

Jolene's heart twisted into a knot. Logically she knew

he was talking about their chances for survival, not any personal spin she'd put on their relationship.

Still, she didn't want this time with Nate to end. With just the two of them to rely on, she'd found strength and wisdom she didn't know she possessed. She'd helped him start the healing process on those invisible wounds that cut him so deeply. They were good for each other. Good together.

But the outside world might prove a tempting lure that could tear them apart. California was part of that outside world. No hurricanes to mess with there. There were prettier, more experienced, less impulsive women in that outside world. Women without babies to remind him of the child he couldn't save. Nate's life would be a lot more sane and safe and predictable away from her.

She'd just hoped that after last night—after yesterday—he might not be so eager to leave their haven. It had probably been a foolish dream to expect a man as responsible as Nate to sit around and wait for the outside world to come to them while he enjoyed what they had for a little while longer.

But she'd dreamed it anyway.

Nate turned the bill of his Rangers ball cap to the back of his head and narrowed his gaze in her direction. "Why are you so quiet this morning? I'm not used to keeping up the conversation all by myself."

"I'm just tired, I guess." It wasn't a complete lie. "You kept me up kind of late last night."

His eyes warmed, reminding her of the tender way he'd been watching her when she awoke in his arms that morning. "Did I ever thank you for that?"

She summoned a smile and nodded. "Twice."

"Thanks," he added for good measure. He righted his cap and untied Checker's reins. "I'd better get going. I have no idea how long this will take. And keep in mind, I'm not asking you to stay because I don't think you're capable of helping me. But there's still work to do here. And I will move faster on my own."

Without her around to make a bad situation worse?

She kept the honest, if uncharitable, thought to herself. "I know you're right. And I am worried about Dad. It'd be a huge relief to hear his voice and know he was all right."

"I'll make that a priority," he promised. "And remember, you won't be alone today. You've got the dogs, the horses, and hey, you've got Rocky. What better company could you ask for?"

Jolene laughed at his efforts to ease her concern. "Your sense of humor needs some serious work."

"Give a man a break. I'm just now learning how to laugh again."

She could see that he was. The grim lines that had etched his face in a perpetually watchful frown when she'd first met him back at the fire station had eased into the hint of a dimple and a lazy grin.

Maybe he'd take a piece of her with him when he went back to California. He might talk about her fondly as that one-of-a-kind pregnant virgin he'd had a brief affair with down in Texas. Hopefully, he'd laugh at some of the predicaments she'd gotten them into.

And she prayed that he'd never know how much it would break her heart to lose him. Because Mr. Responsibility would take that burden of guilt upon his shoulders and let it weigh down his soul. He'd lose his new smile and strengthen his determination never to hurt anyone the same way again.

That's what a man like Nate Kellison did.

It was one of the reasons she loved him.

She clapped her hands together, needing to cut short the gloomy spell and send him on his way before she did something impulsive like tie him up in the house or break into tears. "You'd better mount up, California. You're wastin' daylight."

California. Oh, Lord, she'd slipped.

His shoulders stiffened in suspicion at the nickname. "I'm not going to find you up on the roof or in the loft, am I? Those repairs can wait."

He'd stay if he thought she was in danger, but that wasn't the choice she wanted him to make. Being a burden to him wasn't exactly the romantic future she had in mind. "All my chores will be at ground level. I promise."

"Ground level?" he asked, looking as though he was trying to find a hidden meaning in her words that he'd missed.

She raised her right hand. "No ladders. If I can't fix the well pump, then I'll start hauling water and boiling it. I'll see what's left to do after that."

"Don't haul anything too heavy."

"Go."

"And remember to eat. A couple of snacks besides lunch."

"Nate." She was actually pushing him away now, urging him toward his horse. If he still suspected something was wrong, he hadn't guessed its cause and she wasn't telling. "I'll be fine." His gaze dropped to her belly. "So will he. Now get out of here. Give my best to

Lily when you see her. Tell Dad to get a cell tower hooked up and call me."

Nate slipped his left foot into the stirrup and swung his right leg over the saddle. He was still stiff and sore, but moving with greater ease than he had two nights ago. He adjusted his hat, pulled on his gloves and nudged Checker forward.

He'd shooed the dogs out of the way and ridden beyond the mud pool that had once been her gravel driveway when she saw his posture stiffen. He reined in his horse and turned.

"I'm coming back."

Jolene raised her voice to shout in return. "Of course, you are. I've already got dinner planned. Peanut butter and jelly sandwiches."

He looked at her a moment, then spurred Checker into a spin and rode straight at her across the yard.

Jolene retreated several steps, giving the horse plenty of room to stop. She hid her trepidation behind a joke and a smile. "You don't like PB and J?"

In one fluid motion, he stopped the horse beside her, reached out with his gloved hand to palm the back of her neck, bent low over the horse's shoulder and kissed her. A quick, deep, soul-stealing kiss.

The look in his eyes was just as potent.

"I'm coming back."

He sat up straight, turned the horse and cantered away. Stunned, Jolene pressed her fingers to her mouth and barely breathed. She watched his straight, broad shoulders until he disappeared beyond the next rise.

I'm coming back.

Yes. But would he come back to stay?

THE PICKUP ENGINE sputtered, then caught and roared to life. Red lights blinked on. The noisy crackle of static flooded the cab and the tuner on the two-way radio flashed through every station until it hit a clear frequency and locked into place.

"Way to go!"

"Yessir!"

Nate's relieved sigh was drowned out by a chorus of shouts from three little boys who didn't know what the cheering was all about but who were as excited as the grown-ups around them.

Jolene's sweet green power truck had been hit hard by Damon. Pummeled by debris, the body was totaled. But more importantly, winds had taken the radio antenna and shredded the connecting wires. Water had swamped the engine and shorted out the battery. Since there was no auto repair store on the corner to walk to for replacement parts, Nate had scavenged what he needed from Lily's car and Deacon's old farm truck. With Wes Mathis's help, he'd pieced the engine together and gotten both it and the radio running.

He listened to the voices on the line with the dispatcher in Turning Point. They were connected to the world again. "Whaddya know? The damn thing works."

Deacon slapped Nate on the back, then reached out with his good arm to shake his hand. "You've got a habit of savin' the day, boy. Glad to know you."

Nate nodded his appreciation for the older man's grudging respect.

"Come on, you three yahoos!" Gabe, Jr., Seth and Aaron Browning circled around the old cowboy with an excitement that rivaled Broody and Shasta at suppertime. "I promised your mama you'd be inside taking a nap by now. You don't want to get me into trouble, do ya?" They paraded up the porch and into the house, and Nate suspected Deacon would be napping right along with them.

Cindy threw her arms around Wes's neck and kissed him in congratulations. Nate couldn't help but shake his head and grin at their not-so-private celebration. In the hour since he'd arrived, he'd noticed that the newlyweds didn't need their expensive hotel room in San Antonio to act like a couple of honeymooners. Not that they were doing anything they shouldn't in front of the kids, but they'd grown up and grown closer in the past couple of days.

Like Jolene and Mitch and a lot of other people around Turning Point, he suspected, Wes and Cindy had risen to the challenge Damon had hurled at them and come through the tragedy with plenty to be proud of. And from the number of times they'd found a way to hold hands or sneak a kiss, all squabbles had been forgiven and the two were clearly very much in love.

Nate waved goodbye as they excused themselves for some more intense congratulating. He leaned back in the seat behind the steering wheel and thought of Jolene. The weather had rinsed her scent out of the truck, but he could close his eyes and breathe it in through his imagination. Smells of home and life and laughter.

He could feel her in his body, too. The enthusiastic way she reached for him and held on. The gentle stroke of her fingers across his face.

He could taste her in his mouth. Hot, sweet, willing. Equal parts sass and sugar.

He could see her in his mind. An unruly strand of sun-kissed hair blowing across her cheek. Soft, pale skin. Everywhere. He could see her crying. Arguing. Smiling. Giving herself to him. Healing him.

He could hear her voice and know her soft, gentle words were the truest balm his soul had ever known. He could hear her laughing, or crying out his name at the height of uninhibited passion, and know he'd never experienced any bigger adrenaline rush than the time he'd spent with his angel.

Something hard and stubborn squeezed the breath from his lungs and shattered his restless doubts into a billion pieces.

Nate slipped his hand into his front pocket and fingered the smooth gold ring Grandpa Nate had left him. He knew the warmth he felt in the metal band had to do with body heat and August temps.

But if he thought a little less, believed a little more…maybe the soul he shared with that wise old man was trying to tell him something.

Nate slowly opened his eyes and scanned the devastated Texas landscape. Not so many days ago he'd left California, a man without a home, a man with a heavy conscience. Not quite a whole man. The life he'd put on hold for his family and work had passed him by in Courage Bay.

But he'd found it in Texas.

In the dazzling smile of one blue-eyed angel.

A hopeful energy seeped into his thoughts and spread its renewing strength into his veins.

He needed to think about this.

But not too hard.

The ring practically burned in his hand. "Yeah, I get it. I get it."

Nate smiled, silently thanking his wonderful grandfather, who'd taken him in as a baby and given him the home he'd needed then. But the time had come to find a home of his own.

Hell. He'd thrown every other caution to the wind. Maybe there was something he could learn from Jolene's impulsive nature.

Nate picked up the radio and pressed the call button. The excited dispatcher, Ruth, shouted out her office door. "Mitch! It's them. Mitch!" Then she dutifully took down the information from Nate's report. Half a minute later a door slammed. Ruth's voice grew faint. "Sweetie, they're all right. Nate says they're all right."

He heard Mitch's hoarse voice in the background. "Let me on that line."

There was a flurry of movement.

"Here."

"Thanks, hon."

Then, "Kellison?"

"I hear you loud and clear, Mitch."

"Thank God. How's Jolene? The flooding's bad out your way. Are you safe at the house?"

Nate grinned. Mitch didn't know whether to be boss or father right now. He had a feeling Mitch had done enough worrying for both roles. "I'm at the Rock-a-Bye. I forded a stream along the property line that had gone down enough to be passable. Took us about an hour to get the radio in Jolene's truck working. Jolene's back at

the Double J. Fit and feisty as ever. I don't think even a
hurricane could bring her down."

"That's my girl. Headstrong, but tough."

And funny and sexy and full of heart. And worth
every bruise and bandage on his body. But he couldn't
say that to Mitch. Instead he asked, "How's the damage
there in town?"

"Bad. The ranch?"

"It needs work. New roofs and windows. A shed.
Some steel fencing. When the water goes down, we'll
see if there's anything left of the road, but she'll definitely need to lay a new driveway. And the well. She's
trying to get that running again today."

"My God. And everyone's okay?"

Nate ignored his own battle scars. Mitch had
switched to father mode. He wanted to hear about his
daughter and grandson. Nate quoted the words she'd
told him time and again, even if he hadn't always believed them. "Jolene and the baby are fine."

After a quick accounting of their patients at the Rock-
a-Bye, and a status report on his three friends and fellow volunteers from Courage Bay, Nate needed Mitch
to be a father again. Sitting up straight in his seat, as if
facing the man himself, Nate put forth a proposition.
"When we get back to town, there's something I'd like
to discuss with you, Mitch. I'd be curious to know
whether you'd be interested in hiring a paramedic to
help Turning Point get back on its feet until your doctor comes back. Or even to stay on full-time."

Mitch's ravaged voice was succinct, revealing a bit
of curiosity and suspicion. "You want to move to Turning Point?"

Technically, he wanted to move to a ranch a few miles west of Turning Point. But he wasn't going to ask Jolene's father that kind of question over the radio. Out loud he answered, "Yeah. There's something about Texas that's growing on me. And I imagine you'll be short-staffed for a while."

"I'll think about it. We'll talk later." That was the boss's answer. But Mitch had to make one last fatherly check. Nate respected the man for it. "Everything's all right with Jolene, isn't it? I mean, she's…happy?…With your decision?"

"I haven't really discussed it with her yet."

"I see. Well, I expect my daughter to be safe and happy before we talk about that job."

Nate understood the underlying message. He wouldn't be particularly amenable to anyone who hurt Jolene, either. "Yes, sir." He looked through the cracked windshield and took note of the sun turning into a bright orange ball as it sank toward the western horizon. "I'd better get back to the ranch. She seems to have a penchant for getting herself into situations when no one's keeping an eye on her."

Mitch laughed, the tension eased. "You are getting to know my daughter. Good luck, son."

Nate signed off the radio and turned off the engine. It was time to saddle Checker and go home.

Go home. Nate wasn't thinking California or the rolling, pristine hills of the Whispering Dawn. He was thinking of a few hundred storm-ravaged acres on the Coastal Plain of southeastern Texas.

He was thinking of the blue-eyed angel who didn't believe he was coming back.

HE WASN'T COMING BACK.

The sun was setting, dinner—such as it was—was on the table, but he wasn't coming back.

Jolene wandered through the empty house. She opened the front door, stepped out onto the porch and scanned the southern horizon one more time for any sign of a man on horseback.

No horse. No ball cap. No tight white T-shirt. No Nate.

Only the bellowing cry of Rocky stirring restlessly in his pen. Jolene leaned against a post and watched him walk circles inside the fencing, wondering what he could sense that she could not.

"What's with you?" she teased, as if that big brute would answer her. "Did you get a whiff of some pretty little heifer walkin' by?"

Or did he sense his savior and keeper, Nate, approaching?

Jolene turned and looked one more time. No Nate.

With a huffy sigh that sounded as if she cared less than she really did, she went back inside. She'd kept herself busy all day, doing whatever she could to keep herself from thinking about that California cowboy who could break her heart.

The pump needed a new part, but she'd toted and boiled and bottled enough safe water to flood her own tributary. The house was clean, the yard clean, the horses had been out and the dogs had been brushed and spoiled. Sandwiches were made and a can of soup bubbled over the grill.

Now there was nothing to do but wait. And worry.

Since he'd been gone so long, she hoped he had gotten through to Lily's and wasn't crawling through a ditch somewhere, trying to limp his way back for help. Maybe he'd arrived at Lily's, gotten her truck going, found a decent road and made it all the way into town. Maybe he was already saying goodbye to her dad, making an airline reservation, and asking someone else to drive back and rescue her.

"Stop it." Her imagination wasn't being fair to Nate. He was too responsible a man to completely abandon her. He'd promised he would be back. That last kiss had said... "Oh, to hell with this."

Jolene immediately cringed and patted the baby. "Sorry. Mama's a little stressed. You'd like that nice man to come see us again, wouldn't you? Even if he's just our friend, we want him to—"

The rogue coyote howled outside, its loud, eerie call sending a chill down her spine and raising goose bumps beneath the sleeves of her oversize orange polo shirt. Rocky snorted and stamped the ground. Jolene ran to the door. How close to the house was he?

The coyote cried out again, a mournful and high-pitched howl. She imagined the yips that followed sounded antsy. Unhappy. Hungry.

Then she heard the barking. High-pitched, low-pitched. Fast and furious. Shasta and Broody had sounded the alarm.

"Oh, no." Jolene's breath stopped up in her lungs. "I didn't tie them up."

She heard them out back, heard the yelps and growls. They'd cornered the coyote. Her little terrier and her big baby lab had taken on the hungry, wild canine.

"Stop it!" she shouted, already moving.

Jolene's heart pumped with adrenaline as she finally

pushed her fear aside. She had to protect her babies. Her property.

With a stark clarity of purpose, Jolene ran to the gun cabinet in Joaquin's old bedroom. She unlocked the single-shot bolt-action rifle he'd used as a boy and grabbed a handful of cartridges.

"I'm coming!"

But the dogs were giving chase. By the time she'd loaded the gun and burst through the back door, the barking was fading off to the west. They were running the coyote into the brush, straight toward the drop-off into Livesay Canyon.

"Broody! Shasta!"

Jolene set the gun butt against her shoulder, pointed the barrel into the air and fired off one round. The concussive explosion rang in her ears. But for a moment she held her breath and listened. All was quiet.

Had she scared off the coyote?

But she'd only scattered them for a few moments. The barking started again. This fight was in earnest. "Broody! Shasta!"

Jolene stuffed the shells in her pocket and took off running. With one hand at her stomach and the gun crimped safely in the crook of her arm, she wasn't very fast. But she was determined. The growls and yelps frightened her. She imagined bared teeth and bloody hides. She should have gone back for a horse, but by the time she got one saddled or figured how to get up on one bareback in her condition, one of her dogs could be dead. Or both.

"Broody!" Her lungs burned as she ran. Her heart pounded against the wall of her chest. "Shasta!"

She must have covered half a mile before the pain in

her back demanded she stop to rest. Fighting off her panic, she propped her left hand on her knee and bent at the waist, searching for a position to relieve some of the pressure on her back. "Why don't you crazy dogs listen to me?" she whispered on a wheezing breath. Even her whistle sounded breathy and lame. "Why won't you come back?"

Unable to summon the dogs, she loaded another round into the rifle and fired it off. Silence followed. Jolene strained to hear any sign of the dogs over the heartbeat pounding in her ears. She was closer to the canyon than the house now, out in the middle of treeless brushland. Even with the sun going down, she should be able to spot Broody's big body moving through the carpet of patchy brown grass and brittle tumblebrush.

There.

Jolene whirled around as a creature darted through the underbrush. She could tell by its size it was not one of the dogs. She shouldered the gun and aimed at the spot. Her finger had curled around the trigger before she remembered the firing chamber was empty.

Quickly she dug another cartridge from the pocket of her jeans and prayed that the animal dodging from cover to cover couldn't run faster than she could load the darn rifle. "C'mon." Finally the cartridge slammed into place. "'Bout time."

She raised the gun.

A violent howl, almost like a child's scream, pierced the air. It was too high-pitched to be the lab. "No." Snarling followed. "Shasta?" Ignoring the twinge in her back and the burning in her chest, Jolene took off toward the sounds. A squeal. A bark. Something almost like a hiss. "Shasta!"

Jolene followed the cloud of torn shrub branches and splattered mud. She spotted the wheat-colored coat of the coyote and the blur of black-and-tan terrier nipping at its heels. The two animals circled round and round, their tussle taking them ever closer to the edge of the canyon. Did she fire another shot into the air to break up the fight? Or take aim and risk hitting her own dog?

"What do I do? What do I do?" How did she rescue an overzealous guard dog whose opponent was twice as big and could snap his neck in two? The coyote tried to run, but Shasta was too tenacious for his own good. She watched in horror as the dog gave chase. "Let him go."

The flat, scrubby landscape dropped away into nothing about twenty yards ahead of them. Livesay Canyon. A big, empty ditch carved out by eons of erosion that Nate said had been running water the past couple of days.

The coyote might not be their greatest enemy.

"No—no, no." A different sort of panic shot adrenaline into Jolene's legs. She set down the gun and ran. "Shasta!" Without stopping, she tried to whistle. "Come here. Shasta, come!"

But there was no command she could give, no promise of treats that could stop the dog's instinctive territorial drive. The drop-off loomed before her, growing wider and deeper with every step. "Don't do it," she whispered, gasping in air. "Don't…"

She could see it coming. The tragedy she couldn't prevent. Wild predator. Unforgiving landscape. The good-hearted dog who got himself into trouble because he wouldn't listen.

The similarities to someone else she knew weren't lost on her.

With the devilish imp nipping at his heels, the coyote turned and struck. Jolene gasped and stumbled to a halt, feeling the yelping cry shiver along her spine as if she'd uttered it herself. "Shasta!"

From out of nowhere, the third member of the party dove into the fray. Broody charged to the rescue of his little pal, his big paws beating on the mud-packed earth with the thunder of horse's hooves. He lunged at the coyote.

The next few seconds passed by in a blur of images. Shasta on the ground. Livesay Canyon like the dark slash of a scar. Broody and the coyote, a mesh of teeth and claws.

The two combatants were poised now at the brink of the canyon's lip. Both canines struggled for balance, teetered and spun as Jolene raced toward them.

"Broody!" she screamed.

Falling to her knees at the canyon's edge, Jolene thrust out her hand and snatched at Broody's black collar as the animals tumbled over the drop. "Gotcha!"

The coyote rolled down the incline, hit a ledge and popped over, out of sight. Jolene gripped the leather collar with both hands and tried to brace herself as Broody struggled to scramble up the muddy embankment.

But it was too late. She was too close to the edge. The dog was too big. Jolene felt herself falling forward. Broody went first, and with her fingers still gripping his collar, Jolene was jerked down the steep slope behind him.

She didn't remember screaming. She didn't remember crying out her baby's name. She tumbled and rolled down the sharp incline onto a rocky ledge.

And then she stopped.

Her lungs burned, her body ached. She had one hand on her belly, one still clinging to Broody's collar. The big dog was on the ledge beside her, scrambling on his haunches to find a secure place to sit. A splashing sound caught her attention and she saw the coyote crawl out of the creek on the opposite side from them. After shaking himself dry, he trotted away, free and unharmed.

Still fighting to catch a breath, Jolene lay flat on her back and gazed up at the beautiful stripes of orange, lavender, pink and gold that marked the sunset sky.

Amazingly she hadn't hit her head in that tumble. But she was tired and afraid.

It just felt easier to close her eyes.

She wanted Nate.

CHAPTER TWELVE

GUNFIRE?

Nate's blood ran cold.

"Oh, no. I didn't want to hear that."

He'd dawdled on the ride home, acting like a goofy young man on some kind of romantic mission, stopping to pick black-eyed Susans that had survived the storm.

"Son of a bitch." He cursed himself for forgetting who he was and why he was here. "Jolene!"

Knowing he was too far away to be heard, he shouted her name anyway, hoping against hope. He dug his heels into Checker's flanks and urged the big horse into a gallop. "Jolene!"

Had that damn bull gotten out and threatened her? Was there an intruder? Hell. He'd left her alone. She'd had the saddest look in her eyes when he'd left. And though she'd flashed a game smile, her hopeful, energetic warmth had been missing from the tone of her voice.

She'd thought he was abandoning her. Like her mother. Like her husband. Jolene Kannon-Angel could give happily-ever-afters to everyone she met, but she didn't believe in them herself.

"Hell." He should have said something. Done something. His instincts had warned him of her doubts. That's why he'd gone back and kissed her. His heart had been trying to tell him something even then. She'd needed a promise of some kind. He'd felt the need to do it, but his brain just couldn't get around the idea of something permanent after only three days.

And now that he'd shut off his sensible side and listened to his heart for the first time in his life, it might be too late to give her that promise.

They topped the rise that opened up onto the Double J homestead. With daylight fading and the electricity still out, it was hard to make out anything beyond the buildings themselves. Was that Rocky moving in his pen? Why weren't the dogs running out to greet him?

He reined Checker in to a trot. "Jolene?"

A second gunshot exploded in the air to the west.

Nate whipped the horse around and followed the deadly sound. "Jolene!"

As Checker ran, other sounds reached his ears above the pounding of hooves and jingle of tack and leather. Barking. Snarling. A woman shouting. Jolene.

Then he heard a scream that cut straight to the bone.

Crazy Texas woman! "Jolene!"

They were charging right up to the rim of a shallow canyon. Where the hell was she? Why couldn't he see her? "Jolene?"

He reined Checker to a sudden stop, tossed his bum leg over the saddle horn and jumped to the ground. Nate cursed when he hit. The impact jarred through his knee like the stab of a hot knife blade. But the pain was good. It cleared his head and made his senses sharp.

Dropping the reins to the ground, he limped toward the canyon edge at an uneven trot. He saw Shasta first, lying on the ground like a sphinx-dog, licking at a gash in his front right shoulder.

"Shasta?" Nate spared a moment to kneel down beside the beat-up terrier. Beat-up was right. "I know the feeling, boy."

The cut needed a stitch or two, but wasn't bleeding profusely. The dog had a few other nicks, but his eyes were clear and he welcomed a scratch behind the ears. Nate scanned 360 degrees across the horizon. "Where's your mama, boy?"

Then he saw the gun.

The blood rushed to his feet, leaving Nate light-headed for a moment. "Oh, God, lady."

He picked up the rifle. He could guess who'd been behind the trigger. "Jolene?"

He didn't want to see what he might find, but Nate forced himself to walk right up to the canyon drop-off. "Oh, God. Jolene? Angel, can you hear me?"

There she was, lying flat on her back on a four-foot-wide ledge about ten feet down. No doubt unconscious or worse. Broody sat calmly beside her and looked up at him.

"Hey, boy." Nate acknowledged the scratches and brambles in the lab's tan coat and knew that the dogs had done something very brave to save their mistress. And she'd done something equally brave to save them.

Nate lay down on his stomach and tried to reach over the side to her. Nowhere close.

For half a second, he considered climbing down the slope after her. But the descent was too steep, the ground crumbly and loose from all the rain, and his leg too unreliable.

"Jolene? Angel? I'm coming for you, sweetheart. I'll be right back."

"Nate? Is that you?" Her eyes popped open, bright and clear and oh, so far away. Her precious mouth curved into half a lazy smile. "I was just thinking about you."

"Are you hurt?" Relief, giddy and miraculous, washed through his veins. "Please don't tell me you're down there taking a nap."

His heart couldn't take it.

"Nope. I fell." She pushed herself up on her elbows, wincing in such pain that Nate's body jerked in response. "Don't move."

But she pushed herself all the way up into a sitting position. She slipped her arms around Broody's neck. "You okay, boy? You brave, big thing, you."

She was using that soft maternal voice that got to him every time. "Something might be broken. You know you shouldn't be moving."

Tipping her face up to him, she smiled. "I am a medic, Nate. I just had the wind knocked out of me. Don't get me wrong. It hurts like heck. I feel like I've been thrown from a horse. But I'm breathing fine. My vision's clear, my temperature's normal, and my head doesn't hurt." She braced her hand against the curve of her belly, anticipating his next question. "Joaquin's rollin' around like always. He was the first thing I checked. No unusual pains. No blood. No cramping."

Nate wanted to believe. But there was a smudge on her face, scrapes on her arms. Her ponytail had come loose and bits of dirt and grass clung to the tangled mess. "I should still get you to a doctor and check you out." She reached back and rubbed at the small of her back. "Jolene?"

"How about I trade you one trip to the doctor for a massage?"

"You'll get both," he insisted. If she could wheel and deal and try to sweet-talk her way around his common sense suggestions, then she wasn't as seriously injured as he'd feared. But she was still ten feet away. He needed to get his hands on her and see for himself if she really was in one piece.

Nate scrambled to his feet, giving directions every step of the way. "Don't move. I'm going to lower a rope down to you. Tie it in a good square knot beneath your arms and I'll use the horse to pull you up."

Working quickly and efficiently, he gave her a length of rope, then hurried back to tie it securely to Checker's saddle. "Ready?"

"Ready."

Nate mounted up and urged Checker back. The rope pulled taut, but moved easily without getting caught. A big black nose and lolling red tongue appeared over the lip of the canyon. "Jolene!"

He dismounted quickly and pulled Broody to safety, then untied the rope around him. Of course, she'd rescue the dog first. Couldn't let Nate go down after him. Couldn't come up together. Temper brewed with admiration.

Stubborn Texas woman.

This time he watched until she had the rope securely tied around her. "Use your legs to brace yourself if you can, so you don't get dragged against the wall."

She nodded her understanding. Nate checked her twice before climbing onto Checker. "Ready?"

"I'm ready."

He backed up the horse. The sun was half a ball of

quivering orange heat by the time he spied the crown of that golden hair.

Nate dismounted, secured the horse and ran to pull her the rest of the way himself. His anxious fingers fumbled with the knot. When he had her loose, he led her several feet away from the canyon's edge, checking bones, pupil reaction, her even gait and anything else he could along the way. Only when he was reasonably certain she hadn't suffered anything more than scrapes and bruises did he stop.

"Thanks. I really appre—"

Nate stopped her words with a kiss. Her lips softened and yielded under his. He came up for air and peppered her face and ears and temples with probing, grateful kisses.

"I need to call my vet, Dr. Arkin. The dogs ran off a coyote—"

He silenced her again, slipped his arms around her waist and pulled her tight against him. He felt the press of the baby and eased back a bit.

"You know, I didn't panic," she said. "You told me you'd come back and—"

He kissed her again, and her lips parted in answer. Their tongues tangled and his breath came hard and fast as relief and passion and every other emotion he'd been too afraid to indulge came rushing forward. Her fingers were in his hair, knocking off his cap and angling his mouth this way and that.

Her throat was humming by the time she braced her palms against his shoulders and pushed against him.

And the stitches.

"Ow!"

She looked up at him in some kind of shock. "You came back."

Nate brought his hands up to the sides of her neck and buried his fingers in her hair. He gave her a loving little shake and poured out his desperation. "I said I would. I gave my word. But I can't spend the rest of my life worrying about what fool scrape you're going to get yourself into next time I'm not around."

She shrugged, not getting it yet. "I had to save the dogs."

"Save me, damn it! Just save me!"

His harsh, ragged plea echoed across the storm-beaten plains and settled somewhere in the hopeful light that sparked in those true blue eyes.

"What?"

"I love you, Jolene." He slid his hands down her shoulders, along her arms and back, trying to knead some understanding into her. "But, you know, I've still got a couple of hang-ups that you're just going to have to learn to live with. If you want to keep me around, you're going to have to stop saving the world and scaring me to death that I'm going to lose you and this baby every time you get it in your head that somebody needs you. I need you."

"You need me? You love me?"

That light was blazing now.

"Yeah."

Nate waited, heart and soul wide-open, for some kind of response.

"I love you, Nate Kellison." His name. Her voice. "I love you."

Before the smile had reached his lips, she threw her

arms around his neck and kissed him. Hard. Deeply. Thoroughly. It was an embrace full of the love that had reached into his dark old soul and given him life again.

"Wait a minute." Jolene drew back a bit. "What about California?"

"What about it?" He nuzzled the side of her neck, refusing to release her.

"That's your home."

Nate pulled away and looked her in the eye so she could see just how serious he was. "*You* are my home. *You* and this baby are where I belong. Somebody's got to raise him with some common sense—keep an eye on him in case he turns out to have a heart as big as yours."

"Your family—"

"—can get along without me. They've been getting along without me for a while now. I just didn't know it was time to move on. I still love them. I'll still want to visit." He tucked that errant tendril of hair behind her ear. "But, angel—I had to come all the way to Texas to find you. Here." He reached into his pocket and pulled out Grandpa Nate's ring. He slid the large gold band onto her index finger and kissed it. "Now that I have, I intend to stay."

And with that declaration, she covered her mouth and burst into tears.

"Aw, geez."

"Hormones," she sniffed.

He cradled her in his arms and rocked her gently back and forth. "Crazy Texas woman."

"Crazy about you."

HARLEQUIN®
INTRIGUE®

WE'LL LEAVE YOU BREATHLESS!

If you've been looking for thrilling tales of
contemporary passion and sensuous love stories
with taut, edge-of-the-seat suspense—then
you'll love Harlequin Intrigue!

Every month, you'll meet six new heroes
who are guaranteed to make your spine tingle
and your pulse pound. With them you'll enter
into the exciting world of Harlequin Intrigue—
where your life is on the line
and so is your heart!

THAT'S INTRIGUE—
ROMANTIC SUSPENSE
AT ITS BEST!

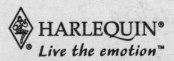

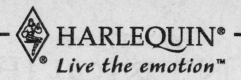

HARLEQUIN®
Live the emotion™

Upbeat, All-American Romances

flipside

Romantic Comedy

Harlequin Historicals®
Historical Romantic Adventure!

INTRIGUE
Romantic Suspense

HARLEQUIN ROMANCE®
The essence of modern romance

HARLEQUIN®
Presents
Seduction and Passion Guaranteed!

Emotional, Exciting, Unexpected

Temptation

Sassy, Sexy, Seductive!

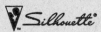

From first love to forever, these love stories
are fairy tale romances for today's woman.

Modern, passionate reads that are powerful and provocative.

Emotional, compelling stories that capture the intensity
of living, loving and creating a family in today's world.

A roller-coaster read that delivers romantic thrills
in a world of suspense, adventure and more.